THE FESTIVE LOVE COACH

TOYA RICHARDSON

The Festive Love Coach

Published: Toya Richardson
Editor: Karen Sanders
Cover Design: Francesca Wingfield
Formatting: Pink Elephant Designs

ACKNOWLEDGMENTS

I'd like to say a massive thank you to my editor, Karen Sanders. I have learned so much from her so far. I am grateful for her professionalism, support, and friendship. Karen, I couldn't do this without you.

Huge gratitude to Francesca Wingfield for the most amazing cover. It's perfect!

To all my readers old and new for taking a chance on my work, you guys are amazing. I have also been blessed with some fabulous friendships on my writing journey. Thank you from the bottom of my heart for your continued support.

SPECIAL ACKNOWLEDGEMENT

Without an hilarious Facebook post I saw from a reader about her experiences of a Christmas coach trip, this story would never have come about. Beverley Ann Hopper, much gratitude for sharing your coach trip experiences with us. If not for you, I honestly do not think I'd have ever come up with a romantic comedy. Thank you so much for all your love, friendship, and support. I love you, lady!

This book is dedicated to the memory of my amazing and beautiful mum, Anne Colleer Tebby, who I miss every single day. She taught me how to use my imagination and follow my dreams. I love you, Mum.

CHAPTER 1

MAYA

Maya breathed a sigh of relief as she closed her laptop and grabbed her coat. Her boss had generously let her go at midday. Excellent news for her. It was her last day of work before setting off on her skiing trip with boyfriend, Stu. Now she would have plenty of time to pack for their early morning flight the next day. She had high expectations for this holiday. Hopes that he would finally propose to her. He'd been acting very mysteriously recently and had a secret smile on his face.

She elected to head over to his flat to surprise him, and with any luck, get a little loving too. After parking up, she grabbed his spare key out of her bag and headed upstairs to the first floor. A grin spread across her face at the surprise she'd see when he saw her. As quietly as she could, she let herself in.

After taking off her shoes and coat, she headed for the lounge. The TV was on, but no one was in there, or in the kitchen either. There were two wine glasses and a bottle of red on the kitchen counter. Maybe he'd guessed she'd be leaving work early. A noise from his bedroom distracted her. Perhaps he was already packing. Then she heard a distinctly feminine giggle.

"Oh God, Janie. That is so good."

Maya stopped dead in her tracks. Janie? What was his business partner doing in *her* guy's bedroom? Fury rushed through her a mile a minute and she saw red. She burst through his bedroom door just in time to get slapped in the face with a pair of black lacy panties. The naked couple faced her, shock registering in their expressions. Janie hid under the duvet and Stu cupped his junk. Watching him do that would have been comical at any other time. Hell, she'd seen it on countless occasions.

"Stupid question, I know. But what the hell is going on here?" Maya demanded.

"It's not what you think," he moaned, grabbing for his boxers.

"Oh, really? It looks like you're having sexy time with that bitch cowering under the sheets. What is it if not that then, huh? Doctors and nurses? Mummies and daddies?" She threw her hands up in the air. "You know what? I'm done."

She stormed out of the room, trying to control the fast-flowing tide of tears springing from her eyes. He ran after her and grabbed her arm. Maya shoved him away.

"Don't. You. Dare. Touch. Me, asshole!"

"Be reasonable!"

She laughed at his audacity. "Really? *Me* be reasonable? Are you saying I should just pretend I didn't see you screwing your *business partner*?"

"What about our holiday? You'll still go, won't you?"

Her body shook with rage and shock at his question. "NO! I will NOT go with you!"

Stu moved towards her, and for the first time, she wondered why she'd ever thought he'd be a perfect boyfriend, or even husband, material. She realised she still had her handbag clutched tightly. On instinct, she pulled back the arm holding it and then swung it at him, hitting him square in the nose, which poured with blood. He crumpled to the floor, clutching at his nose.

"Ow, that hurt," he whined. "I bet it's broken."

"Tell someone who gives a shit. Get Janie to wipe it better with her smelly panties. Happy fucking Christmas!"

Fetching her coat and shoes, she headed for the front door. She remembered the key to his flat and turned to throw it, where he still sat on the floor, clutching at his nose. Janie, the cowardly bitch, had yet to emerge from his bedroom.

"Here," she said, throwing the key back at him. "I won't be needing this again. Give it to the slapper hiding in your bed."

Maya slammed the front door shut; the sound echoed loudly in the hallway.

MAYA

When she got home, she flung herself down on her sofa and sobbed until she gave herself a headache. At thirty-two, she thought her life was all planned out. Stu had put paid to that. She headed for the freezer, fishing out a tub of pralines and cream ice cream. With her free hand, she grabbed a half empty bottle of wine from the fridge. After she'd eaten most of the frozen dessert and emptied the wine bottle, her thoughts turned to how she'd spend her holiday what did she do now?

They were due to go to the Alps until the end of December, and she'd booked two weeks off. It hit her that she'd be alone for Christmas. It was usually her favourite time of year, and that deceitful ass had ruined everything. Her sister, brother-in-law, and their kids had gone to his brother's family in Florida. Her parents were spending the time at their villa in Spain. Maybe she could stay with her mum and dad. She decided to contact them on Skype. Even her best friend wasn't contactable, off on some hiking holiday with her boyfriend somewhere in the back of beyond in South America.

"Oh, Maya," her mum said as she related the incident to her parents. "We never liked that man. But I'm so sorry it ended this way. And at Christmastime, too."

Maya had an inkling they'd never taken to him but had tolerated him for her sake.

"Do you think I could come and stay with you? I have two weeks off," she asked.

Her dad gifted her with a smile. "Of course, love. Let us know when you've booked your flight, and we'll come get you from the airport."

After several hours of searching for flights to Spain, she realised it was going to be too late to book anything before Christmas. She'd even tried looking at flights to other countries, thinking she could hire a car and drive through Europe. No luck. Nada. Slamming the lid of her laptop down with frustration, she resigned herself to the fact she'd be like the song by Mud, *Lonely This Christmas.*

"Guess it'll be turkey dinner for one then." She sighed.

MAYA

The sound of her phone beeping woke her. Her neck ached and she realised she must have fallen asleep on the sofa sometime after delivering the disappointing news to her parents. Grabbing her phone, she stared at the screen through gritty eyelids. Numerous missed calls and voice messages from Stu. She deleted everything without looking and blocked his number.

After a shower and copious amounts of black coffee, she headed into town. She didn't have anything in the fridge because she wasn't going to be home. It was the twenty-first of December, so still time to get perishables. And several bottles of wine to numb the pain of being cheated on.

Before going to the supermarket, she visited her favourite coffee shop for a gingerbread latte and a mince pie with cream. Nothing like junk food to soothe the soul. The shop was full of groups of people with bulging shopping bags. Couples, families, friends, all chatting excitedly about the forthcoming festive holiday. Her spirits sank lower. She couldn't help but be jealous. Thoughts turned to Stu. God, if she hadn't turned up unannounced, how much longer would their sham of a relationship have continued? A shudder ran through her as she tried not to contemplate how long the affair had been going on.

Tears swam in her eyes, more out of anger than anything else. She brushed them away with the back of her hand and went to get up.

"Hey, careful!"

Too late, she heard the deep male voice call out in warning. The next thing she knew, she'd knocked a large mug of coffee out of a hand. It made a loud clatter as it smashed on the tiled floor. The shop went silent. All eyes on her. Could her life get much worse?

"Ouch," the same male voice said.

Glancing up, she saw an expensive light brown coat now covered in black coffee. Her eyes travelled farther up and collided with a pair of deep sea green eyes. She imagined they'd usually be smiley; at that moment, they swam with irritation.

"Oh my gosh, I'm so sorry," she babbled, reaching for some serviettes to try and clean the coat.

"It's okay. No harm. No foul. Just watch where you're going next time."

She wasn't certain if he was angry or simply taking the mickey out of her.

"Yeah well, I have a lot going on in my life," she mumbled and grabbed her bag, embarrassed to see most of the people in the café were still watching them. "Sorry again."

Maya scurried away, tears blinding her eyes.

MAYA

After her humiliation with green eyes in the café, she headed for the shops to gather up all the goodies for Christmas that she could carry. If she was going to be miserable over the festive period, she may as well do it with her favourite foodstuffs.

Once her food mission was complete, she strolled down the main road. She came to a halt outside a local travel agent's shop. There were various offers, but one that caught her eye for some weird reason. It read, *"Due to late cancellation, there are now two seats available on this fantastic festive trip."*

Reading the details underneath the main ad, she saw it was a hotel in Eastbourne, departing on 23rd December, back 2nd January. There was a reduction of two hundred pounds. Coach trips weren't usually her thing, but it was a steal.

"What the hell. Better to be with a coach load of people than on my own."

She strode through the door with purpose.

CHAPTER 2

CARTER

Carter was fed up with his married friends trying to farm him off to single women. He was sick and tired of the endless rounds of blind dates with women who didn't do anything for him. It was one thing to meet a woman organically. That way, he'd choose to be with her because there was a connection. Dating the other way was mostly awkward and unfulfilling, having nothing in common with them apart from being alone.

He didn't want to spend the festive season with anyone this year. He'd lied to his family. The guilt weighed a little heavy on his shoulders, but he was fed up of witnessing the sympathy in their eyes. They thought he was going on holiday for the festive season. He just had to hope that no one saw him. The previous relationship he'd had with Leanne turned out to be an unmitigated disaster. She'd left him for a man five years his junior. Still, no use dwelling on the past. It was done now.

The scent of coffee on his coat still lingered after the brunette with amber-coloured eyes had knocked it all over him. He'd been certain she was angry initially, but as she'd turned to leave, he was positive there were tears in her eyes. Now, why was that? He shook his head. Why should he know or care?

After ordering another coffee and drinking it in peace, he left the shop. Carter had just put one foot on the zebra crossing when he heard the loud screech of tyres. He jumped backwards in shock, landing on his backside. When he got up, he saw a car half over the crossing. He was filled with astonishment when his eyes locked onto the driver. Familiar amber eyes stared back in horrified surprise.

"Jesus, not again," he muttered.

Sitting behind the wheel of the car was the woman who'd spilt coffee all over him a short while before. Her mouth opened and closed, but no sound came out. Jesus, his day was turning out to be a barrel of laughs. Carter sauntered to the driver's side and indicated for her to wind the window down. He leaned in.

"Are you seriously trying to kill me? Has someone put out a hit on me?" He didn't know whether he was tormenting her, or just plain irritated.

"Like I said, I have a lot on my mind. I'm sorry. Again." She turned away to face the front.

He huffed out a breath. "Yeah, well, maybe you should leave the car at home next time, in case you kill someone."

Her eyes narrowed and her breathing elevated. She turned her face back to him. "Tell you what, next time I see you crossing the road, I won't stop and just mow you down. How's that sound?" She rolled up her window and drove off at speed.

"Christ, woman. Take a chill pill." He shook his head.

When he crossed to the other side, he took a quick glance in the travel agent's window. Perhaps it would be a good idea to see if he really could get a last-minute getaway. Someplace warm would be perfect. It was so close to Christmas Day, but there might be something available at a reduced price. At least it would get him away before anyone spotted him.

After about an hour of discussing various options with one of the travel agents, Carter came away with his travel documents in hand. He looked at the itinerary and shook his head. This was either going to be the trip from hell, or a good surprise. Either way, it was a last resort and fairly cheap. And who knew, maybe he'd meet the woman of his dreams. Or, more likely, a lot of mature ladies old enough to be his great grandmother.

MAYA

When she got back home, she slammed the door behind her and threw her car keys and bag down hard on the hall table. Twice. Twice she'd had a run in with some guy. How she hadn't hit him on the crossing, she had no idea. She needed to get her head back in the game before she wound up killing someone for real. His words were heavy with sarcasm, which hadn't helped her sour mood. Her reaction to him was totally out of order, and she knew it. Usually, she was good-natured. Stu had destroyed that, for the moment, at least.

There was a missed call from her mum on WhatsApp. After grabbing herself a cuppa, she sat down and placed a call back to her.

"Hey, Mum. What's up?"

"I was just checking to see how you are, Maya."

"I'm okay. I've managed to book a trip away over Christmas and New Year."

"Do you think that's wise?"

Uh-oh. She had her concerned head on now. Maya pressed the handset against her forehead, closing her eyes to gather her thoughts.

"Mum, I'm thirty-two years old. I'm sure I know what I need to do."

A sigh greeted her down the line. "I know. I just worry. Take no notice of me. So, where are you going?"

"Um, a coach trip to Eastbourne."

The line went silent, and then a chuckle greeted her ears.

"What's so funny?"

"At least I won't have to worry about you being safe, especially from men."

Maya rolled her eyes. She wasn't in the mood for jokes.

"I'm so pleased you find my situation amusing. For your information, it was all I could find. I was lucky to get this at a knockdown price because of a last-minute cancellation. It's not my fault my boyfriend decided to sleep with another woman just before we were due to go away," she finished with more vehemence than she intended.

"Oh, love. I'm so sorry. I didn't mean to upset you."

She sighed. "I know you didn't. I'm sorry too. Only, things are a little raw. As you say, I'm sure I'll be safe from

11

unwanted male attention… apart from old guys in their eighties. I'm sure I can outrun them and their walkers."

They both laughed and the tension was broken.

"When do you go?"

"Day after tomorrow."

After a few more minutes, Maya ended the call. She remembered she hadn't even looked at the itinerary in any detail. Grabbing the travel documents from her bag, she checked what was in store for her…

23rd December Travel to Waves Hotel, Eastbourne. Arrive approx. 5 p.m.

24th December Free time. Resident band in evening. Silly jumper competition at the evening party.

25th December Bucks Fizz reception at noon. Followed by Christmas lunch at 1 p.m.

26th December Day trip to Lewes.

27th December Trip to Beachy Head

28th December Free time.

29th December Day trip to Brighton.

30th Mystery Tour.

31st December Free time.

31st December New Year's Eve celebration dinner and dancing until late.

1st January Free time.

2nd January Depart hotel for home at 9am.

There will be nightly entertainment in the ballroom, which is included in the price.

It was going to be pretty full on and not very restful, but on the free days, she planned to read and walk. She headed for her bedroom and hauled out her suitcase. She chose several warm jumpers, jeans, and trousers. Thankfully, she had a silly Christmas jumper from when her work had hosted a charity day. She held up the bright red sweater which had a ram and ewe on the front kissing. Written in black and silver glittery writing underneath the picture was the slogan, *All I want for Christmas is Ewe.* It was cringe-worthy, but perfect for this competition.

As there was evening entertainment, she picked out a few skirts and blouses. Her eyes skimmed over her dresses and she decided on two as there were parties on Christmas and New Year's Eve. She hung them up, ready to put in her case the following evening.

When the morning of the trip dawned, she was up early so she could have a good breakfast before she set off. She packed her iPod, Kindle, and some magazines in her back-pack. It was going to take all day to get there, and she wanted to ensure she had enough reading material to keep her occupied. She popped her handbag inside the back-pack, along with a bottle of water and some sweets. Checking she had her purse and travel documents, she waited for the taxi to arrive.

When she reached the bus station, she strolled over to stand ten, which was the pick-up point for the coach. There were several people already there. And as she suspected, they were mostly sixty plus in age. A couple, probably in their forties, was also there with two teenagers. She wondered how on Earth they'd enjoy this trip. Judging by their bored expressions, eyes glued to their mobile phones, they wanted to be anywhere but there.

"Oh, boy. This is going to be such fun," she muttered under her breath.

Their coach arrived and she hung back, letting everyone else get on before her. They had allocated seats, so it wasn't a problem. Hers was the window seat the row before the backseat. Maya looked at all the walkers and wheelchairs which had to be loaded. There were more of those than luggage by the looks of it. She was so glad she wasn't the tour guide or the driver. They'd certainly have their work cut out on this trip.

The tour guide ticked people off her list as they got onboard. She gauged the lady was heading towards sixty and she already looked harassed. This was only the start of the trip; goodness knows what she'd be like by the end of it.

When Maya finally got on, she took a deep breath. Most of her fellow travellers were still taking off coats, putting their bags away, and getting settled. She fixed a smile on her face and attempted not to scream at them all to hurry up. One lady was having trouble putting her coat and bag up on the luggage rack. Maya took pity on her.

"Here," she offered, taking the items from the lady. "Let me help you."

The lady smiled her gratitude. "Thank you, dear. That's lovely."

"No problem."

Maya realised her mistake too late. Several others had witnessed her display of kindness and asked her to help them. By the time she reached her seat, she was hot and flustered. There were two more pick-up points before the coach commenced its final journey to Eastbourne. The second stop was, again, mostly elderly people, with one couple possibly in their forties. The seat next to her remained vacant. With any luck, it would stay that way.

By the third pick-up, she'd donned her iPod to drown out all the incessant chatter and had her head in one of the magazines, reading an article about serial relationship cheats. Probably not the best thing to focus on after her recent experience. She hadn't even realised that the coach had stopped until she heard someone placing items in the rack above the seats.

Glancing up as the person took the seat next to her, she couldn't hold back her gasp of surprise. Her eyes grew wide with horrified shock as she met a pair of green eyes that she recognised. It was the guy she'd covered in coffee and almost run over not two days before.

"You!" she said in an accusatory tone.

Green eyes didn't appear to be enthused by the idea of sitting next to her either. This trip was going to be worse than she'd initially envisaged.

CHAPTER 3

CARTER

Carter headed off to meet the coach at its pick-up point and began to question his sanity. This trip was bound to be filled with older people. No one of his own age group. But then again, would that be such a bad thing? At least he wouldn't get hit on by single women. It wouldn't be so bad for him to be with the older generation, especially with his job role. He worked for a local charity as an advisor for the elderly, so it would probably be a busman's holiday for him.

It was why he hadn't been bothered about going on a holiday such as this one. It was his comfort zone. One lady was having trouble negotiating the steps of the coach and he went to her aid.

"Need a hand?" he asked her.

"Would you mind? My legs don't work quite as well as they used to."

"Not at all. Here." He offered her his arm. "Hold on tight."

Once he'd navigated her to her seat, she turned and smiled at him. "Thank you so much, love."

"Anytime."

Carter glanced at his boarding information again and saw he was close to the back of the coach. He'd come prepared with audiobooks, music, and a newspaper. This journey would be a long one, and as most of his fellow travellers were well into retirement age, it was going to be a long time getting on and off, too.

He noted there was a woman sitting in the window seat next to his, engrossed in her magazine. From what he could see, she looked to be more his age. At least he wouldn't be on his own. Carter took the seat next to her. When she looked up, he was faced with a pair of angry amber eyes. The eyes of a woman who'd covered him in coffee and almost mowed him down on a crossing.

"You," she snapped.

"Hey, it wasn't like I expected you to be on this trip. Trust me, lady, if I'd known, I wouldn't have booked this holiday. I value my life."

"What do you mean by that? It wasn't as if I did it on purpose. I'm not in the habit of attacking guys I don't know."

"Oh," he countered. "Just guys you do know, huh?"

For a bizarre reason, he wanted to goad her. Probably not his best idea, especially as they were going to be 'coach mates' for almost two weeks.

"I said I was sorry, and as I told you I…"

He held his hand up to stop her. "Yes, I know. You've got a lot on your mind."

He watched as she drew in a breath and ran her fingers through her hair. Momentarily, he lost his train of thought as he watched her draw her fingers through her silky tresses.

Down, Carter. This is not the line of thought you need. Do not get any ideas about this hellcat. She'll probably string you up by your balls.

She turned to face him, her expression unreadable.

"Look," she finally responded. "We're going to be stuck together for several days, and I don't want any extra grief."

"I couldn't agree more. Let's pretend the incidents from the other day never happened. What do you say?" He smiled at her and held out his hand. "Hi. My name's Carter."

She eyed his hand for long moments, as though weighing up whether she should shake it or not. He wondered why the hesitancy and whether it had anything to do with, 'the things she had on her mind'. Then he took her hand in his. It was warm and soft, and tingles shot up his arm. Now *that* was unexpected.

"Hi, I'm Maya. And once again, I'm sorry for the other day."

By the way her eyes widened, she'd experienced something, too.

"Good to meet you, Maya. And please." He waved his hand in a dismissive manner. "That's all in the past now."

After their introductions, she buried her head back in her magazine. Her iPod was fixed to her ears. Even though they had a truce, her actions told him that she clearly wasn't in the mood for conversation. He put on his headphones and listened to one of his audiobooks.

MAYA

Maya couldn't believe her bad luck when Carter sat next to her. What were the chances of this happening? She must have done some really bad things in a previous life for this to occur. Still, he'd been happy to start over and forget her misdemeanours from a couple of days ago.

She had to admit, he was pretty easy to look at. Sea green eyes, short black wavy hair, square jaw, and just enough facial stubble to not be scruffy. Lips that gave the impression he smiled a lot, turned upwards at the corners. Tight blue jeans, a checked flannel shirt, and a black t-shirt underneath. Even the shirt couldn't disguise the fact that there were some pretty well-defined muscles lurking underneath. And what the hell was that shock which ran through her when their hands touched?

Maya shook her head. Those thoughts needed banishing from her mind. She was still too raw after what Stu had put her through. It was also blatantly obvious that they were only being polite with one another because they were stuck in each other's company. At least once off the coach, she could escape. After reading her magazine, she popped it back inside her backpack. Not ready to read anything else, she listened to her music.

Her eyes landed on the seat across the aisle. A couple in their later years sat discussing something. The man picked up the woman's hand and kissed the back of it lightly. She blushed and snuggled closer to him. She caught Maya watching and shared a knowing smile with her. Maybe if she found her soulmate, it would be that way for her too. A wistful sigh came from her lips.

Carter leaned closer to her. Damn, his aftershave smelled good. A tremor ran through her.

"It's good to know some relationships can stand the test of time, isn't it?" His eyes moved to the couple across the aisle from them.

"Hmm, just what I was thinking. I reckon the younger generation could take a bucket full of leaves out of their book. Think things are too easy nowadays. Less scruples when it comes to chea…" She stopped herself.

No way did she want to discuss her cheating ex's habits. Fortunately, Carter had picked up on that and didn't say anything else.

It was time for their first coffee and lunch stop. Maya was surprised at how helpful Carter was with the older folk, chatting and laughing easily with them and helping them with their belongings. He bent to pick something up off the floor, and she had to admit, the guy had a very fit rear.

"Handsome chap, isn't he?"

She blushed when the lady from across the aisle caught her ogling.

"Don't worry, dear. It's natural. My name is Esme, and this is Doug, my husband.

She smiled at the couple. "Good to meet you both. Um… we're not a couple."

Doug had already left his seat and headed to the exit. Maya fell in behind Esme.

"I didn't think you were. Especially by the way you

reacted to one another when he sat down. But you have met before?"

Maya wasn't usually someone who liked to discuss her personal life with strangers. Something about Esme made her more relaxed about it. People were heading in little groups towards the service station. Doug was waiting for them and helped them both to alight the coach.

"Thank you." Maya smiled and made to head off.

Esme touched her arm. "Look, we're not pushy, and if you don't want to then please say no. But would you like to join us for a coffee?"

Maya looked to Doug. A grin covered his lips. He was a handsome man with pale blue eyes and a shock of white hair. She could only imagine how striking he was as a young man.

"I am more than happy to have two beautiful ladies with me. That should set tongues wagging." His smile was warm.

"Okay. Then thank you. I'd love to."

Doug found them a seat and went to fetch drinks. He'd waved Maya's protestations away. "You can buy the next ones."

"I'll hold you to that."

"Now then. I know we don't know one another, but I think you have a story to tell and I'm a good listener."

Before she knew it, Maya had told her all about Stu and her run-ins with Carter.

"So, you can see why I was so shocked when Carter sat next to me. I don't think the fates like me very much." She groaned and rubbed at her temples.

Esme took Maya's hand in hers. "It could be that the

fates, or whatever, are giving you another chance. Maybe a helping hand?"

Doug came back at that point, so their heart to heart was at an end. Her eyes landed on Carter. It appeared he'd been taken under someone's wing too and was happily engaged in a lively conversation with two ladies. She loved how his smile was so genuine and how interested and attentive he was with the women. He must have sensed her watching and his eyes found hers. Her cheeks burned and she turned quickly away.

CARTER

Carter had helped two sisters, Annie and Jean, to get off the coach and he fetched their walkers for them. They were a lively, fun pair who would put the younger generation to shame. He'd watched Maya as she struck up a friendship with the couple opposite them on the coach. With them, she appeared more relaxed and her guard was down. She was quite the beauty when she smiled.

The husband had gone to fetch drinks, leaving the two women deep in conversation. Whatever the topic was, it appeared that Maya was pouring her heart out to the older woman. He speculated as to whether she'd experienced a relationship break-up. He also wondered if she'd told her about their encounters a couple of days before. The older lady had looked over at him with a telling smile on her face. Perhaps she had, who knew? He never could understand women.

He was taken away from his musings when Annie asked him a question. "Are you certain that young lady isn't with you?"

"Absolutely. Why do you ask?"

The old lady looked at her sister and they tittered. "Because you seem to glance at one another quite often. Or you have since we've been in this café."

Had he really been watching her that much? The tour guide came in the café and began to gather everyone up. *Saved by the bell.*

"Come on, ladies. Let me escort you back to your seats."

Carter was about to sit down on the coach when Esme tapped his shoulder.

"Would you mind if I sat with Maya for a while, young man?"

He shrugged. "Of course not."

As soon as the women were settled, they began talking in earnest. It appeared Maya was quite taken with the older lady, and vice versa. It was as if they'd known each other for years. And now she was focused on something other than her upset about Carter being on the coach, everything about her seemed to relax. A nudge on his arm tore his gaze away from her.

"Esme can talk for England, son. This way it'll give my ears a rest."

The two men laughed. After a while, Carter became drowsy and nodded off to sleep. He was looking forward to getting to the hotel now so he could shower and chill before dinner.

CHAPTER 4

MAYA

There were two more short comfort breaks. It became apparent that one person in particular was always late back. Lisa, the tour guide, became quite flustered about it. Maya wondered if this was her first ever trip as a tour guide. On the last break, she was almost in tears as she couldn't locate the lost passenger anywhere.

"Here, let me go and check to see if he's in the loo," Carter volunteered.

"Are you sure you don't mind?"

"Of course not."

Maya watched him go. He had an easy style of walking, and she was mesmerised by the swing of his ass in tight jeans. Again. Whoa, this really did have to stop. Esme nudged her.

"I know what you're thinking," she whispered conspiratorially. "It's mighty fine, isn't it?"

"You're so bad, Esme." Maya chuckled.

A few minutes later, Carter came back with Sid. "Found him," he announced.

She had to chuckle because he'd caused quite a stir when he'd first stepped on the coach. He wore a sweatshirt with *Brexit* on the front. On the back was a picture of Boris Johnson and the slogan, *I support Brexit*. Maya wasn't into politics, but the anger of some of her coach mates made her chuckle. They certainly were a feisty bunch and not afraid to voice their opinions.

He led Sid back to his seat and proceeded up the aisle to sit back with Doug. Esme nudged Maya again. She turned to face her newfound friend, who was stifling her giggles. As one, they looked directly at Carter and burst out laughing. The confused expression on his face made it worse, and they laughed harder.

"What?" he asked, as he retook his seat.

"I wouldn't ask if I were you, Carter. Women are a strange breed," Doug cautioned.

By the time they reached Eastbourne, it was heading for five in the afternoon. It had begun to rain. Maya was ready for a long, hot soak in a bath, followed by dinner and an early night.

"Ladies and gentlemen, would you please remain seated until I come back with your room keys. Staff are available to assist you with your luggage should you need it."

Maya stretched and yawned.

"It's been a long day, hasn't it, love?"

"Hmm, it really has."

Lisa came back on with a basket full of envelopes, which she handed to people once she'd ticked their names off the list.

"Ah, Miss Singleton and Mr Jones. Here you go."

Lisa held out one envelope to them. Carter took it from her and raised his eyebrows in question.

"We're not travelling together. I think there's been some mistake. Would you mind checking with reception, please?" he asked, handing it back to Lisa.

Maya noted her harassed expression returning.

"It's okay, Lisa. See to everyone first and make sure they're taken care of. It's not a problem," Maya assured her.

"Thank you."

Once everyone had their keys. Maya and Carter waited until everyone else had got off.

"We'll see you both later." Esme smiled at them. "I hope they sort it out for you."

"I'm sure they will. See you later." Maya waved at the couple.

Once everyone had got off, she and Carter grabbed their belongings and headed inside. The lobby was festooned with tinsel and Christmas decorations. A large tree stood to one side with flashing lights, a lopsided fairy sat at the top. Christmas music played softly in the background. The last of their coach party was being assisted to their rooms. Lisa stood at the reception desk, looking more flustered than before.

"Oh, that doesn't look good," Carter said by her side.

"Um, Miss Singleton. Mr Jones."

"Please call me Maya."

"And I'm Carter."

"There's no easy way to say this, but I'm afraid the travel agent has made a mistake. You both booked late and on the same day. It was a cancellation and… and…"

The dominoes started to fall as Maya realised. "The

previous booking was for two people travelling together, right?"

She heard Carter swear softly beside her. "There are other rooms though, surely?"

Lisa shook her head slowly. Tears swam in her eyes. "There is another coach party in for the same amount of time. I'm afraid they're fully booked."

Maya's heart sank. This was not happening. *Please let me wake up and realise it's all some horrible dream.*

"So, what you're saying is that we have to share a room? Two strangers. A man and a woman. And we have to be in the same room for over a week?" Carter's voice rose an octave or two.

Lisa nodded, more big, fat tears swimming in her eyes.

"Can you at least confirm that there are twin beds in this room?"

Carter stared at her in shock. "Are you suggesting we do this, Maya?" He spread his hands wide.

"Excuse us for one second." She grabbed his arm and led him to one side. "Look. I'm not thrilled about this situation either. But short of one of us sleeping in the bar area or on the coach, what else can we do?"

He huffed out a long breath. "This is ridiculous."

"Don't you think I know that?" she hissed. "The only other option is to go back home. You're welcome to go if you want. But I'm staying put."

"The idea is nuts. Hell, you've already tipped coffee over me, almost mown me down, and now this? What if you sleepwalk and try to kill me? Or put a bloody pillow over my head!"

Maya's anger was steadily rising. "I am tired. I am

hungry and way too pissed to deal with your childish antics. Plus, Lisa is about to have a nervous breakdown. You're more than welcome to sleep in the lobby or the coach for all I care, but I am heading to the room. Trust me, I am too tired to think about murdering you."

Carter's green eyes were raging like a stormy sea, but she wasn't about to back down. After a while, he sighed once more and nodded. They walked back to reception.

"Okay, there's nothing we can do about this. We'll have to accept." Maya felt much better for saying that once she saw relief flood Lisa's eyes.

"Thank you. Thank you both so much. I am truly sorry. I'll make sure the company reimburse you both for the inconvenience. Let me show me to your room."

It was on the top floor. There were two storeys, plus some rooms on the ground floor. They took the lift. If Maya had possessed a knife, she'd have been able to cut the atmosphere in to ribbons.

"Here we are," Lisa announced brightly. "Oh, and I think you'll like it."

"Not a cat in hell's chance," Carter moaned.

There was a brass plaque on the door. The words emblazoned on it did little to relieve the tension. It read, 'Love Conquers All.'

"What the hell kind of room has that written on the damn door?" Carter muttered.

Maya had a sinking feeling in her stomach that she knew what they were about to face. Oh, boy. The fates really did have it in for her. She used her card key to enter. Her eyes widened at the sight before her. It was massive. A suite rather than just a bedroom. All decorated in blues and greens. There was a sofa to one side, a desk and chairs, a mini bar, tea, and coffee making facilities and...

"Oh. My. God. You've got to be kidding me," she whispered.

"Shit," came Carter's response.

To one side, there was a king-sized four-poster bed.

"We have to sleep in the same bed?" she asked Lisa, her voice coming out in a strangled squeak.

Lisa could only nod and added with confidence, "Being this large, it'll give you plenty of room. And," she said, darting over towards a massive wardrobe, "there are enough spare pillows in here, so you can put them down the middle of the bed."

"Please tell me this is all some weird ass dream," Maya groaned.

"Hmm, reminds me of a song called *Welcome to my Nightmare*," Carter added.

"Well, I'll leave you to get settled. Dinner's at seven-thirty." Lisa fled through the door, leaving the couple alone.

Carter had yet to move away from the door. Maya left him to have a look at the bathroom. She wasn't disappointed. There was a large shower and a big jacuzzi bath. After a thorough inspection, she headed back to the main room. Carter hadn't budged an inch, still standing by his case. To hell with him, she was going to make the most of this.

"Which side of the bed do you want?"

"Huh?"

"Do you want to sleep on the right or the left-hand side, Carter?"

"How the hell do I know. I'm still trying to process it

all." He raised his hands to the air and let them fall back down by his sides.

His behaviour was rattling her. She was hungry and tired. Plus, she required an injection of caffeine. She strode up to him.

"Let's get this straight once and for all. I'm not ecstatic about the situation either. But there is nothing we can do about it. We just have to make the best of a bad situation. Now, choose a side and I'll make us a coffee. How does that sound?"

He ran a hand through his hair. "I'd prefer something stronger."

"Me too. We could raid the mini bar, but I'd rather wait until we go down for dinner to have something alcoholic. For now, though, caffeine will have to do."

He nodded, hauled his case to the left side of the bed, which was good for Maya as she preferred the right. As he went through the motions of unpacking, she fixed them a drink.

"Sugar and milk?" she called out.

"I take my coffee black, please. I thought you'd remember that."

Maya chose to ignore his remark relating to the coffee incident of the other day. She left hers on the table next to the kettle and took his to him. Her foot caught underneath a rug by the side of the bed and she lurched forward. Carter grabbed the coffee from her before she covered him again.

"I'm so sorry. I promise you, I'm not usually this clumsy. I've just been through a rough time lately and my head isn't in the game."

She was concerned he'd be angry with her again. Honestly, if he shouted at her, she'd probably have been reduced to tears after all this stress. He placed the mug down on the table and studied her. His lips twitched and his eyes sparkled with mischief. That was her cue to laugh and he joined in. After the laughter subsided, they sat next to one another on the bed.

"Jesus, you couldn't make this up, could you? It's like one of those awful rom-com movies."

"No, you couldn't. But in my line of work, this would make a great story," Maya admitted.

"What do you do for a living?"

"I work for a small publishing company. I design covers for author's books and do some of the proofreading as well. I love my job."

"Sounds fascinating. You'll have to tap up one of your authors to make this into a book," he teased.

"Yeah, you could have something there. What do you do?"

"This is a bit like being at work for me."

"What do you mean? Are you a carer?"

"Nothing like that. I work as an advisor with a local charity for the elderly."

"Ah, that's why you're so good with the older people on our coach."

He nodded. They drank their coffee and unpacked the rest of their belongings. The wardrobe had ample room for all their clothing. She reached for her nightwear and suddenly felt her cheeks burn. What on Earth would he think about her pjs? They were black and white spotted bottoms, but the top had four Disney female baddies on with the heading, *'Bad Girls Have More Fun.'* Plus, she had fluffy bed socks with pugs on, in case her feet got cold. She hurriedly put them under the duvet.

A distressing thought came to her. "Carter, do you wear pyjamas?"

CARTER

Carter was still trying to get his head around this situation. He didn't normally lose it and was always known for his easy-going nature. But with all the recent events, plus he was dog tired and starving, he felt like he was losing the plot. He was surprised at how calmly Maya was dealing with it. He watched as she put all her things away and tried not to chuckle when he saw what she wore in bed. Her question about his clothing was unexpected.

"I usually sleep naked."

"Oh… oh. I see."

He loved how her cheeks coloured at his declaration.

"Hey, don't worry. I can sleep in my boxers and we have dressing gowns supplied so it's cool."

"But… but what if you roll over to my side of the bed?"

Her eyes went wide, and her blush deepened. She really was stunning, and her lips were so plump and kissable. He needed to stow those ideas.

"We'll do what Lisa suggested and put pillows down the middle."

She nodded and glanced at her watch. "Okay. It's six

o'clock. Do you mind if I take a quick bath? Or would you prefer to use it first?"

He smiled. "Go right ahead. Would you like me to make you another coffee? I could put some brandy in it out of the mini bar if you like. Might help with the shock of our situation."

"Coffee would be great. Thank you. No brandy though. Not before I've had something to eat."

"Right, cool."

He began making the drink and she fled inside the bathroom with her dressing gown. The click of the lock sounded. She obviously wasn't taking any chances. After all, they were virtual strangers.

CHAPTER 5

MAYA

After pinning her hair up on top of her head, she poured bubble bath in the tub and filled it almost to the brim with water. She worked out the settings and sank down inside it, sighing her contentment. The bubbling water massaged her tired joints, which ached after sitting for so long. There wasn't time to wallow for too long, unfortunately, as Cater would need the bathroom.

Maya reflected on the events so far. It really was like something out of a rom-com movie. Only in the movies, there was always a happy ever after outcome. This was different. Carter was *not* someone she wanted to be involved with, no matter how hot he was to look at. Stu had burned all her trust away with his antics.

She let the water out of the bath, quickly dried herself, rubbed in her body lotion, and donned her dressing gown. It was fortunate they were in the bridal suite because she wasn't certain they'd have dressing gowns in other rooms. When she left the bathroom, Carter was already wearing his dressing gown.

"It's all yours." She inclined her head towards the bathroom door.

"Thanks."

When she heard the shower running, she strolled over to the wardrobe.

"Hmm, what to wear." She tapped her finger against her chin.

Finally, she decided on a light blue jumper and a navy skirt. She teamed it up with thick black tights and black ankle boots. After putting light make-up and clear lip gloss on, she was ready to go. Now, did she wait for Carter, or did she leave? She elected to wait for him.

"That power shower was amazing."

Maya turned at the sound of his voice. Her eyes bulged and her mouth went slack. He stood in the doorway, with steam all around him. His hair had been towel-dried and was slightly mussed up. That wasn't what caught her attention, though. He stood with his bath towel tied low on his hips. There was a small sprinkling of chest hair and a happy trail which led underneath the towel. The man was ripped. As he dried his torso with another towel, she could see the outline of something moving underneath his other towel.

No. No. No. Stop looking.

A bemused smile ghosted his lips. Bugger. He'd noticed her ogling him.

"Glad you enjoyed it," she mumbled, turning to the bed where she rummaged around inside her handbag. "The bath was sublime too."

Carter walked past her, grabbed some clothing from the wardrobe, and headed back to the bathroom. She caught the scent of his shower gel; it was woodsy. For some reason, it comforted her.

"Maya?"

She turned to face him. He was leaning his hip against the doorframe.

"Yeah?"

"You look lovely."

Then he was gone, leaving her in stunned silence.

CARTER

While he put on his black jeans and a matching sweater in the bathroom, Carter reflected on the way Maya had eyed him. He wasn't stupid, he saw the appreciation in her expression. Why he wasn't annoyed, he didn't know. This woman was accident prone around him, but something about her drew him in. She was vulnerable, he already knew that. When he heard the jacuzzi bath bubbling, he had a fantasy image in his mind of joining her. Well, there was enough room for two.

"Carter, what the hell is wrong with you?" he groaned.

Ten nights of torture sharing a bed with a woman who looked mighty fine. This was going to be a struggle. He wondered if she might have gone down already. It was a surprise to see her still in the room. She sat on the sofa, punching furiously at her phone. From where he stood, he could see tears glistening in her eyes.

"Everything okay?"

Her head shot up. "I'm deleting some pictures, that's all. Are you almost ready? It's just gone seven."

"Yeah. Hang on. I need to grab my wallet."

Carter wanted to know more, but it wasn't his place to ask. As they headed for the bar area, the sound of many voices melded together. Most of their coach mates were there, apart from Sid. No surprise there. He laughed softly. Maya came to an abrupt halt in front of him. Instinctively, he put his hands out to prevent her from falling. They landed on her hips. A tremor ran through her.

His head moved of its own volition until his mouth hovered close to her ear. "Steady. This is getting to be a habit," he teased.

She stiffened at his words, pulled his hands away, and turned to face him. Her amber eyes flashed first with anger and then something else he couldn't quite decipher.

"What's so funny?"

Her harsh tone was like a slap to the face. He had to rescue this situation. Fast. "Sid."

"What about Sid?" She frowned.

Uh-oh. Her hands were now on her hips.

"He's the only one from our coach party not here."

She laughed. Thank God for that. Situation saved!

"Maya. Carter."

Esme's voice broke the tension. She was standing up, indicating that they should join her. Doug, Jean, and Annie were with them. There were also two empty seats.

"Looks like our babysitters are watching out for us," Maya joked.

"Hmm, I guess so."

"You both look lovely. Are you settled in? It appears that

the six of us are at the same table for our meals. We've checked the seating plan." Esme smiled at them.

Knowing they were all on the same table was good. Their coach mates were lovely, fun people. Easy to talk to. He noted the parents with the teenagers and the other couple in their forties were drinking heavily already. With any luck, they wouldn't become too rowdy.

"What do you want to drink, Carter? I'll let you fill everyone in on our *situation*," Maya said.

"Okay. A pint of lager, please."

He watched Maya head for the bar. She looked so relaxed as she interacted with others from the coach. When she laughed, it softened her whole demeanour.

"So," Jean asked. "What have we missed?"

Carter proceeded to fill them in on the fact that he was sharing a suite with Maya. The looks they shared between one another weren't lost on him. They obviously hoped this would bring them closer together. Absolutely no way. He became distracted as he watched her at the bar. Maya leaned in closer to place her order. The barman engaged her in conversation, and they shared a joke. It was clear he was interested in her; he could see the gleam in the man's eyes from where he was seated. Plus, there were a couple of men, possibly from the other coach party, who took more than a passing interest in her.

"Jealous?"

That one word from Esme made him jump. How long had he been studying her?

"No, of course not. She's a single woman. And I have *no* claim on her. Maya can date who she pleases."

"If you're not bothered, why do you *sound* jealous?"

"Did I?"

Esme tittered. "Yes."

Maya headed back to the table and all talk of whether he was jealous or not was cut short.

MAYA

The barman's unwanted attention had almost worn Maya down. He hadn't made much of a secret about the fact he'd like to *show her the sights* during her stay. Yeah, right. The only sights he'd show her would be in a bed. Then she caught sight of two other guys appraising her. This was beginning to get on her nerves. At least sharing a room with Carter might keep them all at bay. Esme was in deep conversation with him. Goodness knows what she was plotting and planning.

"Thanks," Carter said when she placed his drink down. "You okay?"

He'd obviously caught her annoyance.

"Unwanted attention." She inclined her head over towards the bar area.

"Oh, I see."

She took a sip of her pink gin and tonic. The others were busily chatting, going through the itinerary of their holiday. An idea came to her.

"Look, Carter, I need to ask you something."

"Fire away." He leaned closer to her, resting his hands on his knees.

"I came on this trip to get away from a particularly

nasty relationship break up. I don't want to go into the details. But the last thing I want to do is date… or have any unwanted attention." She stared with meaning at the men leaning against the bar.

"I understand that all too well." He sighed.

Now, what did that mean?

"I seem to have acquired some male interest."

"Hmm, I could see that."

There was a hint of something in his tone. Possession? His green eyes went to the guys who'd been watching her and then to the barman. Interesting.

"As we're sharing a room, would it be okay if I said that we're…" Was she really going to suggest this?

"Dating? In a relationship?" he answered for her.

"Well, that's what I was thinking. But if not, I'll understand. It's a dumb thing to say really. Sorry, yet again. Hell, all I seem to be doing lately is apologising." She ran a hand through her hair.

To her surprise, Carter took her free hand and squeezed it gently. "That's fine, Maya."

"Really?"

His mouth curved into a gentle smile. "Absolutely. But I need you to promise me one thing."

"What?"

His green eyes sparkled with mischief. "You promise not to try and kill me again or cover me in hot liquid."

She relaxed a little and laughed, shaking the hand he held out for her. "Deal."

CHAPTER 6

MAYA

She woke with a start, wondering where she was. Her eyes grew accustomed to the space around her. Gentle breathing close by made her sit up. Then she remembered. She was sharing a room with a stranger. For ten nights. The line of pillows down the middle of the bed was still in place, but she noted one of Carter's legs was over her side. Grabbing for her phone, which was on silent, she saw the time was almost seven-thirty. Time for a quick run before a shower and breakfast.

Creeping from the bed so as not to disturb him, she hauled her running gear from the cupboard and headed for the bathroom. Once dressed, she pulled her hair in to a ponytail and went downstairs. The frigid air of the winter morning hit her head-on. It was what she needed to clear her frazzled mind. The hotel was right on the seafront, which was a perfect setting. One or two others were already out jogging along the seafront. Donning her iPod, she set off to run along the seashore.

It wasn't long before she felt warm. The music flooded

her brain and the coolness of the air relaxed her. It was a good way to relieve stress and tension. Not to mention her stiff limbs after a day of sitting on a coach. Her thoughts reflected on the previous evening. It had been better than she expected. Jean and Annie regaled them with stories of their previous coach trips, which had them all laughing.

Esme and Doug had been married for fifty years and Maya loved that they glanced at each other often, smiling with love. Their love was beautiful to see. She made a mental note to ask Esme at some point what their secret was. And then there was Carter. Well, he'd been a gentleman who kept the conversation going too. Fortunately, no one mentioned the room situation after the first revelation of it.

When they'd returned to their room, it hadn't taken long for her to get changed and turn in for the night. She was so tired that her head hit the pillow and sleep had followed almost instantly. She thought she'd heard him say goodnight but couldn't be certain.

Maya had reached the pier and paused to admire the magnificent structure. She'd read that there was a serious fire a few years back. It certainly looked well-maintained now. After breakfast, she'd head back down to take a proper look around.

She surveyed the seafront and all the stunning Victorian buildings. Several were now hotels. Maya realised she hadn't even looked out of the window of her hotel room to see if they had a sea view. Not that she'd been in the right frame of mind to check. It was a shame they'd arrived too late for the Christmas market. She loved nothing better than a good browse.

Right then, she should have been skiing in Switzerland. She'd been with Stu the year before and had loved strolling amongst the Christmas stalls, the scent of glühwein and cinnamon heavy in the air. Tears tumbled down her cheeks.

"No," she mumbled. "I won't be sad."

She headed back along the beach the way she'd just come. Anger, hurt, and the vision of Stu humping his business partner flashed before her eyes. Her breathing became erratic and her tears almost blinded her. She turned up her iPod, needing the music to drown out her emotions. Faster and faster she went until she ran into something solid and slid to the floor. She didn't even bother to look up. Instead, she sat on the damp sand and sobbed her heart out.

Someone knelt beside her. She tore her earbuds from her ears and stuffed her iPod into a small pocket in her top. The scent was familiar. Through the mist of her tears, she saw Carter. Holy hell, why did it have to be him? Now he'd seen her in a weeping mess on the sand. Maya was too weak to move and had no fight in her to push him away as he aided her to her feet.

One finger tilted her chin up. "Hey, hey, Maya. What's wrong? Is it the room situation?"

She shook her head, unable to form words. The concern in his eyes and his gentle tone undid her a little more and she sobbed harder. Carter pulled her against him and held her tightly. He rubbed her back with gentle movements.

"That's it. Let it out."

After a while of being moulded to his hard body, she took a deep breath and moved from him. His hands rested on her shoulders. It was then she noted he was also in running gear, his top now wet with her tears.

"Come on. Let's get you back to our room. I'll make you a hot drink and you can tell me all about it."

He took her hand and led her back to the hotel. She was relieved that they managed to get back to their suite without anyone noticing them. A lot of their party were probably still resting after the long journey yesterday.

And now, she sat on the sofa, holding the drink that Carter had made for her.

CARTER

Carter heard Maya head out the door. He caught a glimpse of her and noted her running gear. The idea of a jog along the sandy beach appealed to him. It was his go-to remedy for tiredness and stress. After a few gentle stretches on the beach, he headed off towards the pier. A woman was coming from the pier and making straight for him, her ponytail swinging from side-to-side. Maya.

It was obvious her mind was elsewhere, and as she came closer; she didn't appear to have seen him or show any sign that she was going to slow. He heard whimpering noises and realised she was crying. Instead of getting out of her way, he braced himself for their collision. When she slid lifelessly to the sand, his heart ached for her.

And now they sat on the sofa back in their suite. He waited for her to open up to him. As strangers, it would be easier for her to share whatever her problem was. Surely it wasn't the situation they found themselves in. He hoped not.

"I'd been dating Stu for almost two years. We had a great life, our own properties, fab circle of friends, and amazing holidays too. We were supposed to be going skiing for Christmas until…" She began to sob, clutching at her cup a little tighter.

"Here, let me take it before it breaks." He grinned.

It worked. A faint smile tilted her lips upwards.

"Thanks."

"What happened?" he asked.

Tears bubbled up and fell from her eyes. Instinctively, he took one of her hands in his. A long breath escaped her.

"I'd finished work early the day before we were due to fly to Switzerland. I thought I'd pop over to see Stu. You know, to surprise him. I had my own key." Her big amber eyes stared off into the distance, as if recalling a memory.

"Maya?" he urged her in a soft voice.

"The surprise was all mine. I heard noises coming from his bedroom. I opened the door to see him having sex with his business partner. I got the hell out of there and never looked back. I felt so hurt. Humiliated. I'd even welcomed that woman and her partner into my home. And there she was, getting her freak on with my so-called boyfriend." A sad sigh slipped from her and she shook her head.

"Jesus. I'm so sorry, Maya."

She fixed her eyes onto his. Damn, those eyes looked like infinity pools a man could drown in.

"I guess I should thank my boss for letting me go early that day so I could catch him in the act. God knows how long it had been going on for."

"Have you spoken to him since?" He had to break the spell of staring into her eyes before he was tempted to do something he shouldn't.

"Nope. I had plenty of texts. I only read the first one. He was more concerned about the holiday than what he'd done to me. I deleted the rest without looking at them and got rid of his voicemails without listening to them. I didn't want to hear any lies coming from his mouth. And then I blocked his number."

"That's rough. No wonder you weren't focusing when we had our encounters."

"Hmm. I'm not normally that clumsy. Although, I soaked your top blubbing all over you. Sorry. Again."

"Hey, don't worry about that. Just glad I was there for you. So…" He changed the subject as he felt the first tendrils of arousal close around them. "This is why you're on the 'golden oldies' trip, huh?"

She chuckled. "It is. My parents are in Spain and my sister is visiting her in-laws in Florida."

They fell silent. He looked at Maya to see her pupils had dilated, and she moistened her lips. No, he couldn't let anything happen. She was vulnerable. He was vulnerable. That could turn out to be a huge recipe for disaster.

"I guess we'd better get ready for breakfast before the oldies eat it all," he joked. "Do you want to come down with me?"

He felt it was better to ask than just presume they'd take all their meals together. They could sit anywhere for breakfast.

"That would be good. I'll let you shower first, seeing as I hogged the bathroom first last night."

"Okay."

"Carter?" she called out as he grabbed some clothes.

"Yeah?"

"Thanks… for being there."

"No problem."

MAYA

As Maya showered, her heart softened a little at how sweet Carter had been with her. It was more than she deserved after the way she'd treated him. The most disconcerting thing was, she felt a kind of connection growing between them. The tension in the room after she told him about Stu had been intense. She'd seen the desire in his eyes. But like a true gentleman, he'd backed away. And yet, it would have been so easy to fall into his arms and let go.

Their four friends were not around for breakfast, so they ate alone. It was mostly in silence, but Maya didn't mind that. It wasn't uncomfortable, more contemplative. She watched on in stunned silence as she observed someone from their coach party take a bag up to the buffet breakfast area and load it with food.

"Oh my God. Carter, look," she whispered and inclined her head over to where the person was grabbing a couple of bananas and shoving them in her bag.

Carter spluttered over his coffee and had to stifle a laugh. Maya chuckled silently.

"The funniest thing," Carter said in between his laughter, "is she's being blatantly obvious about what she's doing."

Maya put a hand to her mouth to hide her giggles. "I know, right? I guess she thinks she's paid for it so she's going to take it."

After they'd finished their breakfast, Maya got up. "That's me all set for the rest of the day."

"What are your plans?" he asked.

"Going for a wander around the town and maybe head down to the seafront later. Have a good day."

"Are you sure you don't want to load up a bag of goodies?" He indicated to where the lady had taken the food.

She laughed. "No, I'll pass on that. But if you want to…" She raised her brows.

"I'm done too. Have a great day."

She felt his eyes on her all the way out of the restaurant, burning holes in her back. Once again, it would have been so easy to invite him to go with her. She didn't need company and wanted to distance herself from Carter, if only for a short while. They'd be eating together that evening and she'd have the back-up of their friends.

Being alone with him was dangerous. Maya was susceptible. She sensed he was too. Although he hadn't said anything, she just knew it. And both of them being in that frame of mind could be disastrous.

It was only a short walk to the town centre, and it would be good to get caught up in the festive atmosphere. The decorations were a blaze of colour. She could only imagine how magical it looked at night. All the shops had Christmas music blaring out, a mix of old and new songs which melded into one noisy mass. Kids were high, the excitement of Father Christmas sending them even more hyper.

The town and the hustle and bustle were a welcome break from the tension which had built up between Carter and herself. It felt difficult to breathe and being away from him gave her a chance to relax. After two hours of traipsing around the shops, she decided to head back to the seafront and have a stroll along the pier.

There were several people from the coach taking in the sea air too. She paused to talk to most of them about the weather and had they recovered from the journey. She saw Sid deep in conversation with Jean and Annie. By the way he was waving his arms about, it had to be about Brexit.

There was a café called Victorian Tea Rooms. A nice pot of tea and a piece of cake would be a great way to tide her over until dinner at seven-thirty. Perhaps she should have grabbed some muffins from the breakfast bar like the other lady. A quick check of her watch told her it was just before two. Plenty of time to indulge.

She took in her surroundings. A huge chandelier dominated the centre of the room. Bright lights were placed at intervals on the beams overhead, and wall lights hung along the sides. Taking a seat by the window, she chose Sussex Tea for One, which consisted of a pot of tea, fresh scone, clotted cream, and strawberry preserve. Maya enjoyed people watching and loved to see the children running up and down laughing, old couples holding hands, and a younger couple paused to share a tender kiss.

"Hi, mind if I join you?"

Carter stood by the table, studying her while she watched the world go by outside.

"Are you stalking me?"

"Hell no." He appeared embarrassed.

"I was only joking. Here." She indicated to the seat opposite hers. "Grab a chair."

"Thanks. So, how has your day been so far?"

"Great. I had a little wander around the town then decided to check out the pier."

"You haven't got very far. Was the lure of a cream tea too much to resist?" His green eyes were dancing with mirth.

"Something like that. And you?"

"Guilty too. Never could resist a scone and a cuppa."

When they were brought their orders, Maya let out a soft squeal of delight. "Look at the pretty teapot."

It was in the shape of a golden elephant.

"You're easily pleased."

"It's just so cute, though."

They constructed their scones in silence. Maya watched as Carter took the first bite and moaned his appreciation.

"This is to die for," he exclaimed.

"I agree. It's yummy."

Carter popped some more into his mouth. He bit in so deep and ended up with cream on his nose, which he hadn't noticed. She giggled at his confused expression.

"Now what?"

"You've…" She giggled. "You've got cream on your nose. And this time, you can't blame me." She was reduced to more fits of giggles.

He wiped at it with his napkin. "Has it gone?"

She nodded, still unable to stop laughing. "Sorry," she said, wiping tears away from her eyes. "Yes, it has."

He surprised her by clasping one of her hands in his big warm hand. Her skin heated at the gentle touch. His eyes had turned a soft, velvety green. Her eyes were drawn to his mouth. Another squeeze made her connect her eyes back to his.

"I don't mind you laughing at my misfortune. I'm just glad to see it's happy tears this time. Not tears of sadness."

Her heart went all kinds of crazy inside her chest. Butterflies took flight in her tummy and her body felt warm and fuzzy. Yet another intimate moment between them. How much longer before it went deeper?

CHAPTER 7

CARTER

The tension between Maya and Carter was escalating. Something about her drew him in. After what she'd told him, he wanted to protect her and tell her everything would be okay. If only she wasn't so pretty, with big soulful eyes, silky-soft hair, and big plump lips which he wanted to taste. Then his thoughts strayed to Leanne and what she'd put him through. Did he ever want to trust his heart to anyone else after that?

"Penny for them."

He glanced at the brunette beauty walking beside him. He hadn't even realised he'd been silent for so long. They were almost back at the hotel.

"Just thinking. That's all." A deep sigh slipped from him.

Maya touched his arm, that one gesture burning right through his coat. "Are you okay?"

He shrugged.

"Come on," she ordered, herding him towards the hotel entrance. "Let's get a cuppa in the room. Then you can tell me all about it. You know, like you did for me."

He wasn't certain he wanted to tell her. But then again, unburdening your soul with an almost stranger was easier somehow. After the drinks were made, they sat on the sofa. This was becoming a habit. A habit he was enjoying more than he should.

"We should call this our counselling couch." She smiled with warmth. "So, what happened to you, Carter?"

"I'd been dating Leanne for four years," he began. "She was great fun to be with. Life and soul of the party. I thought she was my forever partner. We'd been together about three years when I proposed." He laughed bitterly at the memory. "She turned me down."

"Did she say why?"

Maya's voice was so gentle, eyes full of concern.

"Said she was too young to settle down. Apparently, she had a lot of living to do."

"That's a daft thing to say. Just because you're married to someone, it doesn't mean life is at an end. You only have to look at Doug and Esme to realise that," Maya mused.

"I know, right? That's what I said, in a roundabout way. And yes, Doug and Esme are a great example."

"What was her response to that?"

He sighed and ran a hand through his hair. "She said marriage was a dated institution, designed to trap people."

Maya's eyes went wide, and she laughed in surprise. "What a weird thing to say."

"Hmm, my thoughts exactly. Anyway," he continued, "things went downhill pretty fast after that. And she left me for a guy five years younger. I haven't dated since."

"That's awful. I'm so sorry, Carter. Let's hope he gets bored with her and moves on to a younger model."

He laughed. "Karma already caught up with her. He dumped her a few months back. I think because she was still in her late twenties and I'm thirty-three, she thought she was too young to settle down."

Maya nodded her approval. "Let's hope it catches up with Stu too."

"I'm sure it will. I guess this makes us quits now, huh?"

"It sure does. If she thinks marriage is rubbish, she really should take a look at couples like Esme and Doug. I have *never* seen a couple so in love. So in tune with one another. I'm going to have that someday," she announced.

"I couldn't agree more. Leanne always did have stupid ideas."

"I've come to a conclusion, Carter."

"About what?"

"Life is too short to be miserable. I think we should forget about all our crap and make the most of this trip. We'll have fun and celebrate the festive season to the fullest extent."

She stood up. Her enthusiasm was infectious. He got up too.

"So, what's next on the agenda?" he asked.

She skipped over to the wardrobe, hauled a bright red jumper out, and waved it at him. "Silly jumper time!"

He laughed. "Sounds good to me."

MAYA

Maya was still trying to get her head around why Leanne would leave such a sweet person. She was usually, apart from where Stu was concerned, a good judge of character. Carter was one of life's good guys.

"So, what do you think?"

Maya turned around and laughed loudly. "Oh. My. God. I think you're going to win the contest hands down."

His jumper was green and red swirls with a male and female snowman on the front kissing. The slogan read, '*I'm snow in love with you*'. But what made it funnier was all the flashing lights.

"I actually got it from a charity shop," he admitted. "Yours is pretty cute... if a little cheesy."

"Says the man with flashing lights and snowmen on his jumper."

They headed down for their evening meal. Most people appeared to have joined in with the Christmas jumper theme. Apart from Sid, who was sporting yet another Brexit top. The family with teenagers hadn't joined in either, although they all wore matching Harry Potter sweatshirts. It took all sorts. A hand waving caught her attention. Esme stood up wearing a gaudy sequined top with elves on it.

"How was your day?" Esme asked after they'd sat down.

"It's been pretty good actually," Carter announced. "I bumped into Maya at the tearoom on the pier. They do a pretty mean scone with cream and jam, too."

"Hmm, Carter's right. Even if someone got more on his face than in his mouth."

He laughed along with her. It was then she noted that their companions watched them with interest. Her cheeks burned.

Carter coughed. "I'm going to get some drinks before Maya can make any more fun of me."

Maya watched him head for the bar. His ass really was mighty fine.

"What's going on with you two?" Annie asked.

Her cheeks heated even more. "We've both decided to make the most of this trip and have fun. That's all."

Four pairs of eyes didn't appear to be convinced by her declaration.

"What?" she asked.

"Nothing, dear. Nothing." Esme patted her hand.

Dinner was a happy affair with everyone excited for Christmas Day. Maya had never felt this chilled, at least not for a long time. She wondered what Stu would have thought of such a trip. He'd have detested it and probably gone home after the first day. The more she thought about it, the more she realised they were like chalk and cheese. Even if he hadn't been screwing around with his business partner, something else would've happened to tear them apart.

Lisa tapped the mic, standing at the front of the small stage where the resident band usually played. All the chatter died down until it was silent.

"Good evening, everyone. I hope you're enjoying the trip so far. As you know, the Waves Hotel is running a silly jumper contest tonight. The waiters and waitresses moving around you have been taking note and have now decided on a winner."

She undid an envelope and cleared her throat. "Congratulations, Carter Jones. You're the winner."

He stood up and beamed. He headed over to Lisa. "Here's your prize." She handed him a red envelope.

Carter ripped the envelope open and smiled. "Wow, thank you so much. Sussex tea for two at the Victorian Tea Rooms."

After the clapping and cheering had died down, he made his way back to the table. He sat down and handed it to Maya.

"Would you like to be my plus one? I promise not to cover myself in cream again." His eyes sparkled.

"I'd love to. Thank you."

The band started up and people began to spill out onto the dancefloor. Maya was feeling sleepy, and after saying goodnight to everyone, she headed out of the room.

"Going so soon."

Carter had caught up with her.

"I'm not normally such a lightweight, but I reckon the sea air has got to me. Think an early night will be in order. It's going to be a party day tomorrow. I'll save my energy for then."

He was thoughtful for a moment. "Yeah, you're right. Mind if I come up now too?"

"Of course not. Just so long as you're only doing this because you want to, not because I'm tired."

"Promise. Scout's honour."

A waiter stopped them at the doorway. "You cannot pass until you kiss. It's tradition."

Maya's eyes followed where he indicated to a bunch of mistletoe hanging from the top of the door frame. Her cheeks heated when she saw the slight smile curving Carter's lips. Oh God, she was in big trouble now.

Carter took her gently by the shoulders, his eyes fixed to hers. "It would be rude not to follow the tradition, don't you think?"

Her mouth opened, but no words came out. And then his lips landed on hers, caressing them softly. She leaned into him, her arms twining around his neck. It was gentle and tentative. A cough broke them apart. The waiter stood with a bemused expression on his face. Carter still held her by the shoulders. She let her arms drop to her sides.

"Um... I..." She couldn't think of a single thing to say.

Maya stumbled away from him and headed up the stairs.

"Maya. Maya, wait," she heard Carter say.

But she was confused and a little breathless. It may only have been a small kiss, but it had set her pulse racing. What was going on with them? She had to get away from him.

CHAPTER 8

CARTER

Carter didn't know what came over him. When the waiter suggested they kiss, he knew in that moment he wanted a taste of Maya's lips. By the way she tugged at his neck when he'd deepened their kiss, she'd been totally into it too. Then why run? What had spooked her? Perhaps it was embarrassment after being 'caught up in the moment'. She was still smarting over her cheating ex's behaviour as well. This probably left her a little confused and afraid.

He headed for the main bar area. She'd probably need a little alone time. He'd have a drink and then follow her up. After ordering a brandy, he took a seat in the corner. The brandy hit the back of his throat, the sting of the alcohol calming him. Nursing the tumbler between his hands, he replayed their kiss.

"What just happened?"

His head shot up. Esme was standing by a vacant chair next to him. Doug was at the bar. Carter indicated for her to take a seat. After another sip of brandy, he placed the glass back down on the table and gazed at the amber liquid as though it could give him the answers he required.

"You saw the kiss." It was a statement rather than a question.

"Yes. The waiter was doing it to every couple who went past him. It wasn't part of the evening's entertainment. Apparently," she whispered, leaning closer to him, "he did it for a bet."

Carter groaned and rubbed at his forehead. "Great. Just great."

"Where's Maya?"

"Gone to the room. I think she was shocked by our response to the kiss."

Esme cocked her head to one side. "You were only doing what the waiter told you to. Although, your kiss did last a few seconds longer than a perfunctory one."

"I think she may hate me now."

Esme tittered. "Did you force Maya to hold you closer to her?"

"No, of course not."

"Didn't think so. Why would she be angry with you, then?"

"Honestly? I have no idea. So much for a last-minute getaway with no complications, huh?"

"Is that what she is, Carter? A complication?"

His head was buzzing, and his fingers strayed to his lips. Lips which had been fastened to a very soft pair a short while ago. The scent of her vanilla perfume clung to his jumper, almost as if she was still holding him.

"Esme, I have absolutely no idea. We were more enemies than anything before we came on this trip. And then we found ourselves sharing a room. We've even discussed what happened with our ex partners. I sound like a CD on repeat, but you'd never believe it, would you?"

"Well, young man. Whatever is, or not, happening between the two of you, you really need to talk to her. If you leave it like this, it's going to be a very long and awkward trip."

He smiled at Esme, knocked back the rest of his brandy, and kissed the older lady's cheek.

"You're right. I'll see you just before midday tomorrow."

He waved at Doug and climbed the stairs, taking the longer route as he attempted to get his head together.

MAYA

Had she really just flung her arms around a virtual stranger and kissed him? Had she lost her mind? Sharing a room with him was going to be pretty tense from now on. Maybe she shouldn't have run off. The rest of this trip was going to get tricky if they didn't talk about it. Her lips still tingled from his lips caressing hers, his stubble had grazed her soft skin, and his hands holding onto her shoulders had warmed her.

"What were you thinking, you bloody idiot?"

When she saw the waiter next time, she'd give him a piece of her mind. And yet, it wasn't his fault. Maya could've declined. One look at Carter's big green eyes and she was putty in his hands. She scrubbed the make-up from her face and took a quick shower, grateful to Carter for giving her some space to get her head together. After donning her pjs, she headed over to make herself a drink. There were two sachets of hot chocolate, and some short-bread biscuits. Perfect. Just what the doctor ordered.

A knock at the door distracted her. She hoped it wasn't the teenagers from their coach. Apparently, they'd been in hot water that morning for knocking on peoples' doors the night before. Placing her cup down on the bedside table, she marched up to the door. Maya gasped when she saw Carter standing there. Was that a slight blush on his cheeks? She frowned.

"Have you lost your room key?"

"No. I didn't want to just walk in in case you were showering."

That was sweet. She moved aside and let him in. He slumped down on his side of the bed and sighed.

"Hot chocolate?" she asked him.

"Eh, what?"

She smiled at his confusion. "Look. I think we're both a little bewildered. Hot chocolate and a couple of biscuits should help."

"Um, yeah. Great. Thanks."

She busied herself making him a drink and placed it down on the coffee table by the sofa. Then she grabbed her drink and the biscuits and sat on one side. It was probably better there, rather than sitting on the bed. That was just a little bit too intimate after their kiss. Carter sat and nursed his cup.

"The waiter told us a lie."

She raised her eyes to study him. "How do you mean?"

"Well," he said, as he sipped his drink. "Esme informed me that someone had a bet with him. Dared him to do it."

Maya couldn't help but see the funny side and laughed. "The little bugger."

Carter laughed too, then his eyes turned serious. "Do you regret it?"

She ran a hand through her hair. "It was unexpected."

"That's not what I asked," he countered in a soft voice. "Look, I don't want this to cause an atmosphere between us. I'll be honest, I don't regret it."

Maya's cheeks warmed. "I don't regret it either, but I'm kind of confused."

"Me too."

She munched on a biscuit, deep in thought. "Look, Carter. Let's play this by ear. We kissed. Got caught up in the festive celebrations. Let's leave it at that."

He seemed relieved, but she sensed a little disappointment too. She chose to ignore it. Sure, he seemed a great guy, but getting involved was not something she'd signed up for.

"Tell you what, let's raid the minibar. It is Christmas after all, and we're both due some compensation after the room mix up. What do you say?"

Maya got caught up in his enthusiasm. "Sure, why not? Just one though."

The sound of singing woke Maya. Her watch said it was half past midnight. Carter stirred on his side of the bed.

"What the bloody hell is that racket?"

Maya strained to listen and groaned. "It's the damn Birdy Song. God, I hate it with a vengeance." She clapped her hands over her ears.

"Me too. Always reminds me of little old grannies dancing at wedding receptions."

She laughed. "You're right. Love the analogy."

They lay in darkness, listening to the drunken revellers as they carried on humming the tune. A door opened somewhere farther down the corridor.

"I know it's Christmas Day. But please can you shut up?" someone asked.

There were a few drunken apologies and then it all fell silent.

"Happy Christmas, Maya."

She smiled into the darkness. "Thanks. Happy Christmas to you too, Carter."

CARTER

Carter woke around eight, feeling surprisingly refreshed after the disturbed night's sleep. He heard Maya talking softly and realised she wasn't in bed. She was on the sofa, feet curled underneath her. She heard him move and shook her head slightly. It was then he heard someone else and realised she was on FaceTime. He nodded and placed a finger to his lips. He grabbed up some clothes and crept into the bathroom. By the time his shower was finished, and he was dressed, Maya was off the call.

"Hey, Carter." She smiled, still curled up on the seat. "Just had a call with my parents. Will you be calling anyone today?"

"No. I told them I was going abroad and wouldn't get a

good signal. Since the break-up with Leanne, my parents and all my friends have been trying to get me to go and stay with them. I've done it before, and I couldn't stand the sympathetic looks they kept giving me."

"I understand that. I had tried to get a flight to Spain to be with my parents. I'm glad I didn't now though."

"Any particular reason why?"

"My dad would've been great. He always makes me laugh, even when I'm down. My mum would be worrying and fussing over me."

"That doesn't sound so bad."

She smiled at him. "No, I know it doesn't. But one hug and word of compassion from my mum and I'd be crying. Stu took enough from me; I won't cry over him anymore."

"Fair enough. So, are we going down for breakfast?"

"Sure, as soon as I'm out of my jammies."

He was almost tempted to say she looked hot as she was. Carter stowed it though. The last thing he wanted was to cause any extra awkwardness between them.

MAYA

As the six friends sat at the breakfast table, the atmosphere around them was electric. None of them had too much to eat. With lunch at one in the afternoon, no one wanted to spoil their appetite. Maya chuckled and nudged Carter. His eyes followed her line of sight and widened.

"What? No way? Is she selling it on a stall outside the hotel?"

Mrs Hungry, as they'd named her, was up at the breakfast bar sneaking more food into her bag.

"Ah, you've noticed that too, have you?" Esme asked in a conspiratorial voice, leaning closer to Maya.

"We've seen her on another coach trip," Annie added. "She does it all the time."

Jean tutted. "I asked her why she did it the last time. We get well fed on these trips. Her response was she'd paid for it, so she was going to take it."

Maya's eyes landed on Carter's and they laughed. It was a little louder than either intended and the woman glanced at their table, still loading up her bag. After adding another muffin, she mumbled something under her breath and stalked out of the restaurant. After breakfast, the six of them headed out of the dining room and sat in the comfy chairs in the lounge close to the bar.

"I fancy taking a little walk. Shall we all go together?" Maya asked.

Esme and Doug agreed right away. Jean and Annie were a little hesitant. She guessed it was because they were a little slower on their feet. Carter noted the same too and winked at Maya.

"Ladies, Maya and I can escort you back to your room for your walkers. We're only going for a gentle stroll and would love it if you could join us."

Esme concurred. "Yes, we should all go together. We can take in the sea air and work up an appetite for later."

Maya smiled when they agreed.

"I'll get our coats. Carter, I'll meet you at Jean and Annie's room. Esme and Doug, we'll meet you down here."

Maya grabbed hers and Carter's coats. She put her coat

on and clasped his tight to her. The scent of his aftershave and his own signature scent permeated her senses. As she waited outside the sisters' door, she buried her nose in his collar, closed her eyes, and inhaled. He really did smell so good.

"Do I smell that bad?"

Her eyes flew open to see Carter and the sisters watching her with bemused expressions on their faces. The way he looked at her, she realised she had been well and truly busted. How did she extricate herself from this embarrassing situation?

CHAPTER 9

CARTER

He'd just helped the sisters with their coats and manoeuvred their walkers outside their door. What he didn't expect to see was Maya taking a deep sniff at his coat. By the gentle smile on her lips, she was savouring it too. His body reacted as he imagined her mouth at his neck, kissing and inhaling his scent. Oh, God help him. The sisters were deep in conversation, and he broke the spell so as not to embarrass her too much. It didn't work though. Her face burned like a beacon, and the sisters noticed.

"Um, what aftershave do you wear? It smells familiar. I was trying to work out what it was."

Wow, she saved that situation. He was impressed.

"It's Tom Ford Noir. Why?"

"I think it's the one my sister's husband wears. I like it."

He grinned and moved closer to her, snagging his coat from her hands. "Good to know."

Her face was aflame by this time, and her mouth formed a sexy little O.

"Are we ready?" Jean asked.

The spell was broken once more between them.

"Ladies." He ushered them towards the lift.

Maya hung back a little. She'd drawn in her bottom lip and was deep in concentration.

"Maya?"

She shook her head and nodded. "Sorry. I'm ready."

They had a pleasant stroll along the seafront. It took a little longer as their older friends required rest, and they sat on the seats situated along the prom. There were quite a few people taking in the sea air. Carter noted that Maya focused on a conversation with the ladies. She was trying way too hard in his opinion. Being discovered sniffing his coat had embarrassed her. But not him; he was actually glad he'd caught her.

"So, young man," Doug said, as the two of them headed off on their own to let the women talk. "Are you going to ask her out?"

Carter came to a halt and stared at the man in astonishment. "Why would you think I'd ask her out?"

He chuckled and indicated to a vacant seat overlooking the sea. "Because you like each other. But I don't think either of you can see it fully. Not yet anyway."

Carter scratched at his chin, deep in thought. "I'm not sure how she'd take it if I asked her out. We've both experienced some bad relationships."

Doug leaned closer to him. "Look, life is way too short to hang about. You've had bad experiences, so what? Sometimes you have to take a chance on things. She's a lovely young woman and you're a great guy too. It would be such a shame if you didn't even give it a try."

They fell silent and watched the waves rolling in.

"Hey, you two. Time to head back and get ready for our champers and Christmas lunch."

Neither had seen Maya approach them. Her hair was blowing wildly around her face and her cheeks were filled with a light pink blush. Courtesy of the bracing wind and not embarrassment this time. Carter and Doug got up. The older man squeezed his arm as he walked past him.

"Don't forget what I said, son."

"What did he say?" Maya asked with her head cocked to one side. So adorable.

"Ah, not much. Shall we?" He proffered his arm to her.

She giggled and made an awkward curtesy. "Why thank you, noble knight."

Walking along with Maya, arm in arm, was perfect. Everything felt like a jigsaw puzzle being fitted together. But did she honestly feel the same, or was it only because they'd been pushed together into this situation and forced to make the most of it?

MAYA

Something had passed between Carter and Doug. They'd been deep in conversation when she'd offered to go and round them up to get back to the hotel. Doug was doing most of the talking. And she was left to wonder what it was that Carter shouldn't forget. Going back inside the hotel, the warmth hit her full on. She took her coat off in the lobby.

"It's eleven-thirty," Carter exclaimed, showing her his watch.

"I didn't realise we'd been gone for so long. It was lovely though, wasn't it?"

He grinned. "Yeah, surprisingly so."

They headed up the stairs. There were too many older guests waiting for the lifts. Once inside the room, Maya grabbed some things from the wardrobe as Carter did the same. A thought came to her. She paused her rummaging and faced him.

"You want to know something, Carter?"

"What?"

"I realise our reasons for booking this trip may not have been the best. But I'm so glad I came. I'm having more fun than I've had in a long time."

He leaned against the side of the wardrobe, facing her. "And that surprises you?"

"Yeah. It does."

He smiled. "I work with older people. They have so much they can give to us. Wisdom, friendship, funny stories, and advice. They often get ignored and that's so sad."

She had to agree with him. "If someone had told me I'd be having a whale of a time on a UK coach trip, I'd have laughed at them. But this is one of my best trips. And I've made so many friends. Friends I fully intend keeping in touch with when I get home."

He reached out a hand and stroked the side of her face. It was a gentle touch, but one that stoked flames in her belly.

"Does that include me?" he whispered.

"Yes. It does," she said before patting his arm and moving to the relative safety of the bathroom.

She shut the door, her heart thundering inside her chest. This was madness. But perhaps she should throw caution to the wind and enjoy this man's company. There was such an obvious attraction between them. Even if it was only short lived and they never saw each other again, perhaps she should just take a chance. A knock at the door made her jump.

"Sorry, Maya, but if we don't go now, we'll be late. And we don't want Mrs Hungry stealing all the champagne now, do we?"

She laughed. "Absolutely not. Give me two minutes."

She stripped down to her underwear and hauled her turquoise dress over her head. It was fifties style, with a halter neck, fitted to the waist and then flared out, falling just above her knees. She put on her navy-blue shrug cardigan and matching court shoes. After a quick splash of make-up and perfume, she opened the door.

Carter stood by the bed. The expression in his eyes when he saw her sent a tingle of awareness up her spine. And he looked drop dead gorgeous. Black slacks, a fitted white silk shirt which had the top two buttons undone, and a black jacket slung over one arm. He moved to her and took one of her trembling hands in his. He captured her eyes with his and brought the back of her hand to the heat of his mouth.

"You look absolutely stunning," he murmured in approval.

"Thank you. You look good too."

The tension built between them. A thud at the door broke the spell of desire that was building.

"I may have to kill whoever that is," he grumbled.

A nervous giggle left her lips. When he opened the door, Esme and Doug stood there.

"Sorry to disturb you, but we were sent to search for you. Even Sid has beaten you down," Doug teased.

"Sorry. We were talking and lost track of the time," Maya explained lamely.

Esme and Doug appeared far from convinced with her explanation. Maya picked up her clutch bag and followed Carter out of the door. As she walked past him, she was surprised at his whispered statement.

"This is not over, Maya. To be continued."

CARTER

He didn't know where his sudden rush of boldness had come from. There was no getting away from the feelings he had for her though. Part of him wanted to say it was only lust, but he knew better than that. She was fun to be with, sweet, and kind. The way she interacted with their fellow passengers told him she was filled with compassion. And now he'd almost promised her that a kiss, at least, was on the cards for them.

"Hey, where were you?"

He blinked rapidly as he was faced with Maya, who held out a glass of champagne for him. Carter took it almost robotically, his mind still on thoughts of this woman. After a deep sip of the sparkling liquid, he regained his composure.

"Sorry, just thinking about my chat with Doug earlier." He took another sip. "And thanks for this."

"Welcome. Thought I'd better grab you a glass before Mrs Hungry beat you to it. Apparently," she whispered, moving closer to him, "Annie said she's already had three glasses."

"That doesn't surprise me one little bit. She'd better be careful though, or she may pass out before eating her dinner."

"Oh, that would be a tragedy." Maya raised her free hand to her brow in mock despair.

The sound of a gong distracted them from their banter.

"Ladies and gentlemen, time to take your seats for Christmas lunch," the head waiter announced.

"Great. After that walk this morning, I am absolutely starving," Maya said.

They sat at their usual table, and the conversation flowed easily. There was much mirth as they pulled crackers and wore the silly brightly coloured paper hats.

"I've got a tape measure." Maya held it up with a silly grin on her face.

"That's a useful gift. Keep it in your bag. You never know when you might need it," Esme advised.

"What have you got, Carter?"

Her eyes were bright and those luscious lips of hers were curved into an eager smile. Carter rummaged inside the body of the cracker and pulled out a red cellophane fish. Maya giggled.

"I know what that's for," she said.

"Well, I'm glad someone does." He turned it over in his hand.

"No, this is what you have to do. Open your palm and lay the fish flat on it."

Everyone else watched. Clearly, they all knew what it was apart from him. Maya checked the empty cracker again and pulled out a small piece of paper. She nodded her approval.

"Goodness, it's curled in on itself. What does that mean, Maya?" Jean asked.

Maya's amber eyes went wide. "Well, it means..." She blushed. "It means passionate and caring."

Her eyes locked to his and the world around him faded into insignificance while he continued to fix his gaze to her. What he wouldn't give to pull her closer and kiss those tempting lips.

"Here come the starters."

The sound of Mrs Hungry's voice startled him. He chanced a furtive glance around their table. Everyone appeared to be trying too hard *not to* focus their attention on Maya and him. Another quick look at Maya and they laughed.

"Are we missing something here?" Doug asked.

Maya patted his hand. "We'll tell you later."

They were soon tucking into their delicious Christmas lunch. All Carter's naughty thoughts concerning the beautiful Maya would have to be put on hold... for now.

CHAPTER 10

MAYA

The Christmas lunch was delicious. Maya had wondered if it might be a bit of a let-down as so many covers in one sitting usually meant the food wasn't quite up to scratch. Their evening meals were staggered in two sittings. Even Mrs Hungry appeared to be full and didn't even take the spare bread rolls from her table for those who'd had soup for starters.

After dessert, the six of them had their coffee in the lounge area. By the look of their four companions, they'd be heading off for a late afternoon doze. The resident band was going to be playing later in the evening, with a cold buffet for those who were still hungry.

"Right," said Doug, taking Esme's hand. "Time for a little nap. Will we see you all later on?"

Everyone nodded their agreement.

"We'll be heading off too," Jean confirmed. "See everyone later."

"I know we've had champers and a glass of wine with lunch, but would you fancy a brandy?"

Maya smiled. "Hmm, that would go down well. Thank you."

She watched as Carter headed to the bar. He'd taken his jacket off, so now she got the chance to stare at his bottom again. The way his shirt clung to his body gave her even more to look at. He was way too yummy and tempting. It didn't take him long to get served.

"Here," he said, as he handed her a glass.

She took a small sip and let the amber liquid warm a trail from her throat to her tummy. Without thinking, she slipped off her shoes and sighed.

"That feels so much better. I hardly ever wear these shoes, and each time I do, I remember why. They may look the part, but they pinch my toes."

"What you women go through for the sake of fashion."

"I know." She bent down to rub her sore toes.

Carter moved closer to her on the sofa they sat on. "I can give you a foot massage if you like."

She faced him. The expression in his eyes and the lazy smile ghosting his lips burned her. Her face felt warm. A warmth which came from his offer and not the brandy.

"I think people would start to talk if you did that here."

Carter looked around and shrugged his shoulders. "Who cares? Anyway, most people have either gone back to their rooms, or out for a walk." He gestured to the area around them.

True enough, apart from the couple in their forties from their coach, the place was deserted. The temptation was too much. Her toes throbbed as though adding their support for a massage.

"Oh, what the hell." She moved back against the arm of

the seat and Carter took her feet and placed them on his knees.

"Now just relax."

And relax she did. His fingers worked magic on her feet, working out the tenderness until it became a most pleasurable sensation. Her eyes closed and her head fell back against the sofa. All she focused on was Carter's healing hands on her skin. Part of her wanted those hands to move farther up her legs and... What was the matter with her? But she knew why. She was attracted to him, no two ways about it. Before she knew it, she'd fallen asleep, allowing Carter's gentle touch to soothe her.

CARTER

Carter was surprised when Maya said yes to his foot massage. He wondered if she knew that she was moaning softly as he soothed her aching feet. Trouble was, it made him ache elsewhere. It would be so easy to massage his way up her legs, underneath the hem of her dress and... It was fortunate that they were in a public place and not in their suite, or he'd be tempted to take things to the next level.

He smiled when he realised she'd fallen asleep. She looked so peaceful while she slept. His heart beat a little faster while he studied her. Reflections took him to the time when they'd first met. Who would have thought they'd go from enemies to friends? Maya moved and whimpered in her sleep and he decided to wake her.

Placing her feet back on the floor, he squeezed her hand gently. "Maya?"

She woke with a start, eyes wide as she tried to work out where she was. "Sorry. I must have dozed off."

"Hey, no need to apologise. I guess the foot massage worked?"

She smiled. "Hmm, yes it did. My feet feel amazing now."

"Glad I could help. Did you want to go for a walk?"

"That would be good. If I go back to the room now I may well sleep."

"You wait here, and I'll go get our coats." He stood and headed for the stairs.

"Carter?"

"Yeah?"

"Would you mind taking these torture devices back up and getting my trainers, please?"

"Sure. No problem."

Carter would never admit to her why he volunteered to go alone and get their coats. If he was left alone with her, he'd be sorely tempted to kiss her. And if it happened in their suite, one thing may well lead to another. Maya was still smarting over the discovery of her boyfriend's betrayal. He didn't want to take advantage of her. Even though he desperately wanted to have another taste of her lips.

MAYA

She watched him walk away. He had such an easy, confident style of walking that oozed sex appeal. It was fast becoming one of her favourite pastimes. But this was pure fantasy. It was great that they were becoming friends, but when their holiday ended, they'd return to their normal lives. To the real world. She'd never seen him around town before, so chances were this trip would be the last time she ever saw him.

Maya clutched at her chest as though in physical pain. The thought of never seeing him again was already too much to contemplate. There was no way on this Earth she could fall for someone this quickly. She'd heard of insta-love before, but always believed it was a myth. It was all because of the crap Stu had put her through, and with Carter being so kind, her emotions were playing games with her.

"Are you okay?"

Maya looked to see Carter standing in front of her with her coat draped over one arm and her trainers in his free hand. His eyes were filled with concern.

"Yes, I'm fine. Why do you ask?"

He put her coat and trainers down and reached out to stroke her cheek with the fingers of one hand.

"I asked because you're crying."

Shocked at his statement, she noted that when he took his fingers away from her skin, they were wet. She reached for her bag, fished out a tissue, and dabbed her eyes.

"I… I didn't even know I'd been crying. Sorry, just a little emotional, I guess." She stood up.

Carter helped her on with her coat. "I understand," he responded as he did the buttons up on his coat. "It's certainly been a very strange few days for you, and with the stress of what your ex did to you, I'm not surprised you're a little emotional."

"You're right." She popped the tissue in her coat pocket. "Very strange few days. But I'm still enjoying being here."

"Me too." He paused and she could tell he was mulling something over in his mind.

"You've got that expression on your face again. Come on, spill it."

He grinned and then turned serious. "Would you mind if I held your hand while we walked?"

Maya didn't know what to expect, but his request surprised her... in a good way.

"Yes," she responded in a shy voice. "I'd like that."

It was chillier than it had been before lunch. This time, no one was walking along the front. The only noises to be heard were seagulls crying out overhead and the sound of the waves. She shivered against the cold and paused to lean on a railing to look out over the sea. As soon as her hand left Carter's, she felt the sudden loss of warmth. He placed one arm around her, drawing her closer to his firm body.

"Is that better?"

She nestled in closer. "Hmm, much. Thanks."

They stood in silence for a very long time until it was almost dark. The Christmas lights glittered overhead, casting a magical glow over everything they touched. She shivered again and felt his body respond too.

"Think we'd better get going before we catch a chill out here."

"Yes, you're right. Time for a hot drink before the evening entertainment."

She giggled at the dramatic way he said it. "Oh yes, bingo and other silly party games, no doubt!"

They laughed softly together. Then their laughter faded as they eyed one another, the lights playing off their faces. Carter's eyes had turned a dark green, the intensity of them burning Maya from head to toe. He turned so he was standing in front of her, her body pressed back against the railing. His hands went to her shoulders and slowly moved to her hair, brushing it away from her face.

His mouth drew level with hers, his warm breath heating her. Green eyes roved over her face as her heart beat out of control in her chest, tongue wetting her lips in nervous anticipation of what she hoped was to come.

"I want to kiss you," he admitted.

"Then do it." She breathed the words in little more than a husky whisper.

His lips landed on hers, brushing them with a tentative kiss; his hands held her firmly about the waist. Maya's hands trailed upwards until she wound her fingers in his hair, drawing him closer. His tongue breached the seam of her lips and teased hers into submission until she melted into him, moaning her pleasure.

Stubble tickled and teased at her skin; his hands found their way to her hair, which he fisted almost to the point of pain, but she felt more pleasure than anything. His hard body was now firmly pressed against hers as a groan of appreciation rumbled inside his chest. The kiss deepened in its intensity. Tongues lashed against each other, lips pressing harder together. She felt faint and gently pushed at his chest, needing to come up for air.

When they came apart, she rested her head against his chest. He clung to her, breathing ragged, heart thudding so loudly she could feel it even through his clothing. They stayed that way for a long time, her hands clasped around his neck as he stroked her hair. She wanted to purr her enjoyment, feeling like a well-pampered cat.

He took her gently by the shoulders. It was so dark now that even with the twinkling lights, she couldn't see his eyes clearly. One hand stroked the side of her face and she closed her eyes with contentment. A gentle sigh slipped through her lips.

"Are you okay, Maya?"

Her eyes opened wide and she pressed a chaste kiss to his lips. "Perfect. You?"

His teeth gleamed when he gifted her with a gorgeous smile. "Never better."

CARTER

They strolled back to the hotel. This time Maya threaded her arm through his, walking as close to him as she possibly could. He was more than happy with this arrangement. The demand for a kiss had been on impulse, and he was so happy she felt the same way. It did leave him with a lot of questions about where this could be headed, but for now he was content to be in her company. They didn't utter a word until they got back to the hotel lobby.

"I feel a lot better now we've had a walk. The fresh air has woken me up. Plus, the kiss was a pleasant surprise."

Maya's words brought a smile to his lips.

"Best Christmas present ever, as far as I'm concerned." He grinned.

Her face turned serious. He wondered what she was thinking.

"Maya, do you want to talk about it?"

She studied him for long minutes before responding. "That would be good. Not here, though. Let's go back to our suite."

He followed her up the stairs. They discarded their coats and he watched while Maya made drinks. This was really becoming a much-welcomed habit for them. He sat on the sofa and was pleased when she sat right next to him and not the other end. Maya plonked her mug down, took one of his hands, and turned to face him. He waited for her to say what was on her mind.

"This is all so weird. I honestly don't know what to say."

He squeezed her hand. "Take your time. I feel the same if that helps."

She huffed out a breath. "Kissing a guy, let alone sharing a room with him, was the last thing I expected to find on this trip. As you witnessed on that day I assaulted you, my mind was in a mess. What Stu did to me shattered my confidence and trust."

She fell quiet, and as the silence dragged on for too long, he felt he had to bring her back from wherever her thoughts had taken her.

"I didn't expect this to happen either. Honestly, it's scared me a little. We hardly know each other, but we've learned so much about one another and had fun. I think we have a great friendship blossoming between us. And now that has started to develop into something more. Although it's a little unsettling, I'm pleased."

Her big amber eyes landed on his. So full of emotion that it caused his heart to race.

"I'm pleased too. It's only… well. Oh, goodness, this is harder to explain than I thought it would be." She blushed and put her head in her hands.

Finally, the penny dropped, and he understood what her dilemma was.

"Ah. Sleeping arrangements?"

She nodded. "I don't think I'm ready for *anything* that heavy. This won't be awkward between us, will it?"

He leaned forward and pressed one gentle kiss to her lips, moved away, and stroked the side of her face.

"Maya, I find you incredibly beautiful and desirable. But trust me when I say I would *never* take advantage of you in any way."

A sigh of relief came from her. "That's good to know. And for your information, I think you're hot too. And I promise I won't take advantage of you, either."

The tension was broken between them. Carter could only hope that their relationship kept growing. And when they returned home, who knew, perhaps they would continue to see each other.

CHAPTER 11

MAYA

The holiday was flying past so quickly. It was already 30th December. There was a mystery coach trip, but she and Carter had elected not to go. They were going for the cream tea at the Victorian Tea Rooms, which Carter won for the Christmas jumper competition. The wind had picked up, so it was a bracing walk to the pier. She was grateful for the warmth of Carter close by her side. They sat in the same seats they had on their first visit. It was quiet in the restaurant.

"I'm going to be the size of a house by the time we get home."

Carter chuckled as he handed the voucher to the waitress. "You're not the only one. But to be fair, we have been out running most mornings. It should offset some of the excess weight."

"Oh God," Maya moaned as she tucked into her scone. "This is to die for."

"I agree. It's a little bit of heaven for sure. What's your cooking like?"

"Where did that question come from?"

He shrugged. "Just wondering."

"Well," she said, brushing crumbs from her jeans. "I'm pretty good, actually. I find it therapeutic."

"Me too. Nothing like a couple of hours in the kitchen to forget all the rubbish going on in your life. Do you have a signature dish?"

"A couple. My homemade lamb Pasanda, with onion bhajis, Bombay potatoes and naan bread. And I make a pretty mean fish pie too."

Carter moaned. "I'm in love."

"What? With me or my dishes?"

He chuckled and winked. "Your dishes, of course. Do you really make your Indian food from scratch?"

"Yes, I do. So, tell me, Carter, what is your signature dish?"

"Prawn risotto, and I also make a great lasagne. I even make my own pasta." He puffed out his chest with pride.

"Wow, think I'm in love with your food too."

He took her hand across the table and gave it a gentle squeeze. "When we get back home, maybe we should have a cook off."

Maya felt butterflies swarm in her belly at his proposal. "Are you suggesting that we have a proper date?"

"If you would like to see me again." He clutched her hand a little tighter. "Maya, I've enjoyed your company so much. I really don't want this trip to end."

Her head spun at his admission and, suddenly, she didn't want to go home, either.

"I'd like that very much. I'm going to be sad when this trip comes to an end." She felt tears well in her eyes.

"Hey, baby, please don't cry." He moved his seat next to hers and held her close, stroking her hair and murmuring words of reassurance.

After a few moments, she gazed up at his deep green eyes. "You called me baby."

"Sorry, don't you like that?"

"Yes. Yes, I do. Very much… especially the way you say it." What she didn't say was that it sounded sexy. Intimate, even.

They'd only shared kisses up until that point, but Maya wanted more. Needed to feel his bare skin touching hers. By the way Carter was eyeing her, he had the same idea. His pupils were dilated.

"Are you ready to go?" His voice was low and husky.

"Yes, I'm ready." Her declaration about being ready was more than just about leaving the restaurant. It was her admission that she wanted to take their relationship to the next level.

CARTER

It was a quick walk back to the hotel. In fact, by the time it came into sight, they were practically running. He noted their coach was pulling up outside the front. Esme called out in greeting to them.

"Oh shit," he muttered.

"I agree. Double shit. But we can't ignore her. That would be rude."

Carter had to agree with her, even though all he wanted to do was strip Maya naked and caress her body.

"Hello, you two. How was your cream tea?" Esme asked as they walked into the hotel lobby.

"Delicious, as always. How was your mystery trip?"

Doug rolled his eyes at Carter. "Lisa made a mistake with the location and we ended up in Brighton again. Not that we minded, but you can guess what Sid and some of the others said."

Carter could only imagine. Sid, Mrs Hungry, and her husband were the worst complainers he'd ever come across.

"Oh dear. Lisa didn't cry again, did she?" Maya asked.

"No, love, although it was touch and go. We're having a naughty afternoon drink in the bar. Care to join us?" Esme asked.

Carter turned to Maya, who looked both flushed and frustrated. He had to admit that he was feeling the same. How did they get out of this?

"I'm about to FaceTime my parents. Carter's going to speak to them too, aren't you?" The expression Maya drilled into him left no room for argument.

His mind wandered as to whether she'd be this forceful in bed.

"Carter?" she prompted.

"Um, yes. Sure, that's what we're going to do." He felt his cheeks heat at the lameness of his response.

Doug coughed to hide a laugh at their obvious failed attempt to give the couple an excuse. Esme was sharper, her eyes went from one to the other. One eyebrow raised up in speculation. This woman was way too perceptive.

"Well then, we'll see you both for dinner… have fun." Esme winked and followed Doug to the bar.

Feeling the need for secrecy blown out of the water, Carter grasped Maya's hand and headed for the stairs. By the time they reached their suite, they were both breathless and giggling like nervous teenagers.

"You do realise they both know what we'll be up to, don't you?"

"I don't care if you don't." Carter let his gaze rove up and down her body.

Maya returned his heated gaze, setting his body on fire. "No, I really don't."

Carter grabbed Maya and pulled her to him. His mouth crashed down onto hers and kissed her as though his very life depended on it. She moaned into his mouth, her tongue tangling with his. With great reluctance, he tore his lips away from hers and began taking his clothes off. Maya followed suit. With all their outer clothing off, they landed on the middle of the bed, kissing each other with passion.

Maya was pulling his T-shirt out of his jeans and he tugged at the buttons of her shirt. A long, low wail halted their progress. It stopped and then started again. Louder this time.

"What was that?" Maya asked with her hands still holding his T-shirt.

Carter was about to answer her when he heard a man's voice.

"That's right, babe. Ride me like a fucking cowgirl. Gyrate those hips and give me all of it."

Maya's hand went to her mouth to stop her laughter from spilling over. Then the sound of a bed creaking started. Slow at first, but then it picked up momentum. The headboard was obviously right against one of the walls which backed onto their suite. It thudded louder and louder. The woman's wails and the man's grunts were so loud, Carter was certain the rest of the hotel would hear their bedroom antics.

"Jesus, I hope Doug and Esme don't think that's us," Carter said.

A picture on their wall, just about where the headboard in the other room must be located, actually fell off the wall. Carter leapt from the bed and caught it before it hit the floor. By this point, Maya was rolling around on the bed, clutching at her tummy as laughter bubbled out of her. Carter put the picture down and joined her on the bed. Her laughter was infectious. There was one loud shout of obvious elation as the couple reached their peak and then silence.

"Oh. My. God. That was like something out of a bad seventies' porno movie, wasn't it?" Maya stated, wiping her eyes.

Carter chuckled. "Yes. Whose room is that anyway? Is it someone on our coach?"

Maya started to giggle again and nodded. "It's Mrs Hungry. Now... now," she giggled, clutching at her tummy again. "Now I know why she nicks so much food."

He laughed louder and harder. "Yeah. Must be for all the bedroom Olympics they get up to. God, how are we ever going to face them now? I cannot get this nightmare image of her riding her husband out of my mind."

"Complete with cowboy hat and bullwhip!" She put her face in her hands and shook her head.

"Christ, Maya. Now that is yet another image I cannot unsee."

Maya crawled up the bed and buried her face in a pillow, her body shuddering as she continued to laugh. Carter joined her.

"Ow, my tummy hurts," she complained.

"Mine too. I haven't laughed this much in years."

He watched as Maya slipped off the bed and grabbed two bottles of lager from the mini bar. She opened them and handed one to Carter. They clinked the bottles together and drank deeply.

"Um, Carter?"

"Yeah?"

"I know we were about to... you know. But it's kind of put me off."

Carter leaned in and kissed her cheek. "Me too. But that doesn't mean that I don't want you, because I do."

"Me too. And now we know how thin the walls are, we'd better keep things quiet. If you know what I mean."

"I do, baby. I guess it just depends on how much of a screamer you can be." He nudged her side and did a sly wink.

"Well," she responded, her face dead serious. "I do like to voice how I feel."

Carter felt his body harden at her words. His shaft twitched as he imagined her moaning her pleasure out loud. He reached for her, took her bottle away and placed it on the floor next to his. Laying her back on the bed, he hovered his lips above hers.

"Hmm, I'd love to hear you scream. Think maybe we should see what happens."

Her eyes widened. Her pupils almost fully dilated. Cater pressed his lips to hers. This time, he was going to have her. A loud wail filled the air. Not from Maya, but...

"Oh, for fuck's sake, not again!"

Maya snickered. "I don't know about you, but I cannot stand this any longer. Maybe we should get ready early and head down to the bar."

Carter scratched at his chin thoughtfully. "You could be right. If I stay here too much longer, I may well be tempted to bang on the wall."

"Poor choice of words, Carter. Think there's enough banging going on."

He raced over to the wall where he'd rehung the picture, took it off the wall and placed it on the floor.

"I don't want to risk this falling off again."

He watched as Maya got some clothes out for the evening. "Good idea. Let's hope the thin walls can take it. Last thing I want is to come back and find it's come down completely."

MAYA

By the time they were ready to go downstairs, all thoughts of passion had been dashed. The antics of Mrs Hungry and her husband had stolen her 'moment' with Carter. Twice. At least they'd seen the funny side of it. She could still see him rushing to save the picture from hitting the floor. It was the funniest thing ever. She wondered if she should try and write about her experiences on this trip. There was an abundance of people she could ask for help when she got back to work.

They were soon joined in the bar by Esme and Doug. Apparently, Annie and Jean had indulged in fish and chips on the trip and would not be joining them for dinner that evening. Maya had just taken a sip of her wine when Mrs Hungry came in with her husband. She choked and ended up with wine down her front. Thankfully, it was a black top.

"Are you okay, dear?" Esme asked her with concern.

Maya couldn't speak as she proceeded to chuckle. Her attempts to disguise her laughter were futile. Carter turned to see where she was looking, and he too began to laugh. It was fortunate that the couple chose to sit at the far end of the bar.

"Are you going to let us in on your secret?" Doug asked.

Maya told them of their experiences that afternoon, leaving out the part where she and Carter had almost made love.

"Oh, my goodness," Esme exclaimed, attempting not to look at Mrs Hungry.

"Now I'll never be able to look at them in the same way again." Doug chuckled.

Carter got up. "Refill, ladies?"

"Please," they responded together.

Doug followed Carter to the bar. Maya watched how easily they talked, waiting to be served. Not only was she going to miss Carter, but her other friends too. She sighed and blinked back tears in her eyes.

"Oh, love, what's wrong?"

"I've had such an amazing time, Esme. I've loved yours and Doug's company, and Jean and Annie, too."

"And Carter?"

"Him more than anyone. He's such a great guy. We've agreed to meet up when we get back. We both have a love of cooking, so we're having a cook off." She gazed with longing at him.

"Then why so sad? You know we'll keep in touch too, don't you? Our daughters are dying to meet you both."

"I know. But I never thought I'd come away and find lo…" She stopped herself. Was she really about to admit to Esme that she'd fallen in love with Carter?

A warm hand clasped hers. "It's all right to admit it, Maya. I can see it in your eyes. Carter's too. Fate has thrown you together. I say you grab it with both hands and don't let go."

"I'm afraid, Esme. I realise Carter is nothing like Stu. But getting involved with someone so soon after my ex's behaviour. I guess I'm apprehensive."

"Being scared is part of it. The first time I met Doug, I knew he was the one. He told me he loved me on our first date. Part of me wanted to run."

"What did you do?"

Esme smiled and patted her cheek. "I didn't run. I told him I loved him too. Once that's out of the way, you'll feel much better."

Maya knew Esme was right, but it still frightened her to give her heart to another.

"I have another question for you." Esme's eyes twinkled with mischief.

"Uh oh, what now?"

"When we came back from our trip, you two were in quite the hurry."

"Esme, you really know how to make me blush."

"Sorry, love. I didn't mean to embarrass you."

"Well, I know I can trust you. Let's just say that the 'urgency' was pretty deflated once Mrs Hungry got going!"

They both chuckled.

"I think we may be safer back at the bar, Doug. These two are dangerous when they start giggling."

Carter smiled at Maya. And through that smile, she caught sight of another emotion. It wasn't quite at the forefront, but she instinctively knew it was about their relationship. She hoped her expression conveyed the same as his. A hope for their relationship to blossom into something special.

CHAPTER 12

There was something about the way Maya had watched him when he came back from the bar which had spiked his interest. She tried to hide it on his return but failed miserably. With any luck, after dinner, when they were back in their suite, she'd talk to him about how she was feeling.

"That was a lovely meal." Maya pushed her plate back. "Just two more dinners then we head for home."

Carter noticed the catch in her voice at the end of her statement. He took one of her hands and held it tight.

"You're forgetting something." A smile lifted the corner of his mouth at her confusion.

"I don't get you."

"Maya Singleton, have you forgotten about our cooking challenge so quickly?"

Her lips rose in an answering smile. "Ah, the challenge that I'll win, you mean."

"So cocky. We'll see about that." Carter shared a gentle smile with her.

"You two haven't lived until you've tried one of Esme's

home cooked chicken and ham pies. Not to mention her rhubarb crumble and custard," Doug announced with pride.

Carter groaned. "Oh God, that sounds too delicious for words. I've eaten so much, but now you've made me hungry again."

All four of them laughed. Soon after, they headed to one of the tables set aside for the nightly entertainment. The house band was just tuning up. They watched them as they drank their coffee. Esme and Doug were deep in conversation with a couple at the table next to theirs.

Carter leaned across to speak with Maya. "So, have you seen what they're starting off with tonight?"

Maya perused the sheet of paper Carter handed to her. "Ballroom dancing. I don't think so."

"Why not? We've had fun jigging about on the dance-floor on other nights. Come on, it'll be a blast."

"I have two left feet. It'll be a disaster."

"Look, my parents used to teach ballroom dancing. Trust me, I know what I'm doing. Let me lead you."

"Oh," she said, pulling at her bottom lip. "I don't know."

Carter kissed her hand and locked his eyes with hers. "They taught me and my sister when we were kids. Go on. Take a leap of faith."

She rolled her eyes and laughed. "Go on then. But if I trample all over your feet like a bull elephant, don't come crying to me."

The music started up. Carter got to his feet and held out one hand for Maya. She took it and he led her to the dancefloor.

"No one else is up. Everyone is looking at us," she hissed.

"Here come Doug and Esme. Just relax and let me take the lead."

Soon they were dancing around the floor. Initially, Maya's movements were a little jerky and his feet were attacked a couple of times by her high heels. Soon though, they were swirling around the room as though they'd danced together a thousand times before. More couples joined in, and soon the floor became a little crowded.

"Ready for a breather?" he asked.

Her face was flushed and her eyes alive with happiness. "That would be good."

"So," he said after they'd retaken their seats. "What did you think?"

"I actually loved it. It was such fun. Normally I love to have a good old boogie, but there's something about the old-fashioned, structured dances which is much more satisfying. Sounds daft, huh?"

"No, not at all."

They fell silent and watched while other couples glided by. No one crashed into each other, all following the swirling pattern of dance around the room.

"Carter?"

"Yeah?"

He observed a blush creeping from her neck to her cheeks. A thoughtful, yet cheeky expression burned in her eyes. What was she going to say?

"You know you said earlier about you taking the lead?"

He nodded.

"Well, there's something else I'd love for you to take the lead in."

The tension around them had turned heated, the air thick with sexual tension, even though she hadn't said more.

"And what would that be?" His head leaned closer to hers.

She met his gaze head on, her amber eyes turning the colour of dark honey. "Take me to bed and make love to me. Now. Please?"

His body ached and burned at her request. He stood and she did too, taking his hand in hers. No more words were spoken as they headed away from the function room. In the back of his mind he felt he wanted to say goodnight to Doug and Esme, but he didn't want to kill this moment of passion and need.

MAYA

Maya had never been so bold as to ask a man to take her to bed before. With Carter though, this was an itch which badly required scratching. By both of them. Tension was high when he closed the door to their suite behind him and her nerves kicked in. hands trembling while she watched his eyes devour her. He noted her nervousness and gathered her up in his arms.

"Hush, baby. There's nothing to be anxious about."

He moved from her, but only far enough to capture her face between his hands, eyes drifting with much possession over her. His lips found hers and the dance of passion and possession began in earnest. She succumbed to the demands of his tongue to enter her mouth. A rumble of approval came from him as his tongue caressed hers, his lips moving at a leisurely pace over hers. It wasn't enough for her and she moaned, pressing herself closer into his embrace.

Carter broke first. "I want you so much. Take your clothes off but keep your underwear on."

His words turned her panties in to a sodden mess.

"Only if you do the same," she countered in a breathy whisper.

Together, they began to undress. Hands trembling, fingers fumbling as they fought to get out of their clothing in record time. Carter wore a pair of black boxer briefs which did little to hide the bulge straining against the stretchy fabric. But it was the expression in his lust-darkened eyes which almost tipped her over the edge.

He stood in front of her. "Beautiful," he murmured as his eyes devoured her. "Absolute. Bloody. Perfection."

Her nipples burned against her bra and he chuckled when she clamped her legs together. His hands reached for her breasts, cupping them with loving devotion while he thumbed at her nipples through the flimsy fabric. She arched into him, head rolling back at the ecstasy of his tormenting touch.

"I want to take your bra off and kiss your breasts. Will you let me?" His voice was thick and husky.

"Yes. Please, God... yes," she begged without shame.

Her bra landed on the floor as his mouth descended to one and then the other nipple. Shockwaves of desire ripped through her and down to the throbbing ache between her legs. He was relentless as he continued to suckle, nip, and lick each one. Her hands tangled in his hair in an effort to drag him closer to her. She released one hand and ran it down the plains of his chest and stomach until she cupped him. A deep moan rumbled through him with one of her nipples still in the heat of his mouth.

He tore himself out of her grasp, a hand running through his hair. It was such a hot sight to see a man so turned on by her.

"I think we might be more comfortable on the bed." She moved to the four-poster and lay in the middle.

Carter's eyes widened and he was at her side in an instant. He studied her like he'd never get enough of her. His hands blazed trails over her body, raising gooseflesh wherever they went. His mouth crashed to hers, and after leaving her gasping for air, they travelled all over her body. When his mouth left hers, his eyes devoured her body and she whimpered. One hand cupped her mound. He hardly put any pressure on her, but she felt it all the way to her core.

"Do you know how gorgeous you are, Maya? Not just your body, but your mind. I have *never* felt so turned on in my life."

No words came to her, just a whimpering squeal as she squirmed on the bed. He moved down and pulled her legs apart. Fingers hooked in the sides of her flimsy dark blue panties as he pulled them away from her body. His mouth and hands kissed her with tenderness until reaching the apex of her thighs.

Locking his eyes to hers, he inserted one finger inside her, eliciting a loud moan. "So damn wet for me," he hissed.

His mouth came down on her pussy, kissing and licking her outer lips until she was writhing about on the bed. One strong hand gripped her thigh while he put two fingers deep inside her, his mouth torturing her clit until her head spun. She urged him on, pushing him deeper onto her sensitive bud.

"Carter! Oh, Carter, I'm coming..."

Her world shattered as her orgasm swallowed her whole, the aftershocks teasing her until she came back down. He raised his head to look at her, a beautiful smile curving his lips.

"Good?"

"Uh hum, more than good," she murmured.

She watched as he took his boxers off and positioned himself between her thighs, the head of his shaft waiting impatiently against her entrance.

"Are you ready?" he asked with a gentle voice.

"I've been ready since the first day I set eyes on you," she admitted.

Were there tears in his eyes at her declaration? She didn't have time to think as he thrust deep inside her. The sudden connection between them caused them both to groan their appreciation. Maya wrapped her legs around his waist for deeper penetration. Their movements became hurried. More desperate as they sought to reach the heights of pleasure.

For a moment, the world around them stilled. Green eyes boring deep into her amber eyes. And the world came crashing down around them as their climaxes took them to new levels. The sheer experience of sharing her body so beautifully with a man she cared deeply about brought tears of joy to her eyes. And as they came down from their ultimate highs, she knew she'd never feel this sort of intensity or emotion with any other man.

CHAPTER 13

CARTER

When Carter woke the next morning, it was with his arms wrapped around Maya. His face was buried in her neck as she was spooned with her back against his front. She moaned with contentment, still deep in sleep. He tried to remember when the pillows which marked the middle of the bed had disappeared. But caught in the throes of passion, that would have been the last thing on their minds. Reflections of making love with this beautiful woman filled his head and his body came awake, demanding more. Needing more of her soft curves and the desire to hear her cry out his name as she came.

Carter pressed gentle kisses to her neck, his hands heading for her breasts, which he cupped and massaged. A gasp came from her and she turned to face him. Her eyes were slumberous and her lips still a little swollen with all the kisses from the previous night. Her lips reached for his and they kissed languidly. He pressed his shaft against her thigh, and she moaned.

Maya rolled him on his back and climbed on top of

him. No words were spoken, which made the whole experience more erotic. Expressions and touch were all that was required. With her eyes fixed to his, she lowered herself onto him, eliciting a deep groan from him. They began to move with urgency. Carter held her hips firmly and helped her to pick up momentum. It wasn't long before they reached their goal and came, their cries and moans melding together.

Carter rolled her to the side of him, his hands stroking her hair. "Good morning."

"Good morning to you, too." She started to giggle.

"Was it that funny?"

She stifled more giggles and shook her head. "I was just remembering Mrs Hungry riding her husband like a cowgirl!"

She buried her face in his neck and his laughter rumbled up his chest. The laughter faded and he felt her stiffen a little by his side. He lifted her head to see tears brimming in her eyes.

"Maya?"

"Sorry. I'm a tad emotional."

"In a good or bad way?"

A gentle smile graced her lips, and she bent her head to press a kiss against his heart. This only served to make his heart thunder a little bit more than it already was.

"A very good way. This is going to sound so cliché, but I have never felt such a connection when making love before."

Damn, if he didn't just want to cry right along with her at her admission. "Nope, no cliché there whatsoever. Maya, I'm feeling the same as you. Mind blowing comes to mind."

A deep blush stained her cheeks and she put her head in her hands. "You do know Doug and Esme will guess why we left early yesterday, don't you?"

He chuckled. "Yeah, but they'll both be so happy for us."

"How about a shower together before breakfast?" she asked.

Carter watched her rise from the bed. Her gloriously naked body already calling out to him. It was as though she was a witch who'd cast a spell on him. He rose from the bed and followed her.

"Sounds good to me."

MAYA

They headed down to breakfast later than usual. Their four companions had already left. It was New Year's Eve, and they were probably taking a leisurely stroll along the prom. Maya found she was starving, a testament to how much energy she and Carter had used in the bedroom.

"Do you need a doggy bag like Mrs Hungry?" Carter teased.

She slapped his hand. "Cheeky. Do you fancy taking a walk?"

"Sounds good."

Back in their room, she watched as Carter turned on his phone and swore. She went to him.

"Anything wrong?"

He glanced up, looking concerned. "Several missed calls from my mum. She never calls me. I need to contact her."

"Of course. I'll just check my phone too." She kissed his cheek and sat on the other side of the bed.

"Hi, Mum, it's me... Woah, slow down. What? Okay, I'll try and get back today. Is Sally with you? Right, I'll meet you at the hospital."

He ended the call and Maya's stomach clenched with anxiety.

"What is it, Carter? You're as white as a sheet."

"It's my dad. He's had a heart attack. I have to get back. He's stable, but my mum and sister need me."

"Okay. Contact reception and get them to call you a taxi. I'll pack your stuff."

He nodded mutely and did as she said. Maya's heart went out to him. It didn't take long to get all his things together. He'd just ended the call as she packed the last of his belongings away.

"Thanks for doing this."

"Of course. It's the least I could do. When's the cab coming?"

"Ten minutes."

"Do you want me to come with you?" she asked.

"No. I'll be okay."

He was so distracted that it broke her heart. "Come on then. Let's go and wait out the front. You said your mum said your dad is stable?"

"Yeah, probably a warning to tell him to take things easy. He does way too much. But my mum doesn't cope well in these situations. I need to be with her."

"Of course you do. That's what family is all about."

They stood outside the hotel, waiting for the cab to take him to the railway station.

"Bugger, I haven't told Lisa."

Maya took him by the arm. "I'll sort it out. Just concentrate on getting back home. Ah, here's your ride."

While the driver put the suitcase on the boot, Carter took her in his arms and kissed her with such desperation that her tears fell. She pushed gently at his chest.

"Just go, Carter. Stay safe and take care."

"I will. Just you take care too."

And then he was gone. Maya stared after the car for a very long time. It was then she realised with all the drama of that morning that neither of them had exchanged numbers. Although she worried about him getting home and how his father would be, her tears fell freely down her cheeks. How was she ever going to get hold of him again?

"Maya, what's the matter?" Esme asked.

Through her blurry, tear-filled vision, she saw Doug, Esme, Annie, and Jean watching her.

"Oh, Esme, he's gone."

Esme gathered Maya against her and held her close, allowing her to cry.

"Come on, love. Let's get you inside. We'll have a nice cup of tea and you can tell us all about it." Doug smiled with kindness.

"So, you see," she said as she drank tea with her four new friends. "It was all such a rush that we didn't have time to share contact details with each other. I worry about his dad, but I fear I've lost Carter." She sobbed harder.

"No. No, love. You haven't lost him. You only live a few miles apart. I guess you both know where you work, right?" Annie asked.

Maya nodded, unable to speak as her emotions clogged her throat.

"It'll work out. We know it will." Doug patted her hand.

Maya sat close to Esme, who held her as she sobbed. "I never told him how I felt about him."

Esme took her face between her hands and fixed her with an intense stare. "Love will find a way, Maya. Don't give up."

Maya wanted to believe her, but with Carter gone, it was like she couldn't breathe. Memories of the times they'd shared together, from spilling coffee over his coat to making love. She closed her eyes tightly, not wanting to lose her precious memories of him. New Year's Eve was going to be an anti-climax now he was gone.

"The best thing to do for now." Jean pulled her from her musings. "Is to enjoy the rest of this holiday. Carter may not be with you, but remember, you've four more friends here who love you."

Jean's words brought on a fresh wave of tears. "I will. You are all amazing, I'm so glad we met."

She'd keep the smile on her face and see in the new year with her lovely friends. And on her return home, she'd set out to find Carter.

CARTER

The journey home was a hellish one. Some trains had been cancelled and he had to get a bus connection not once, but twice. He'd kept in contact with Sally, his sister, most of the way. His mum had stayed by his dad's bedside.

"He's going to be okay," Sally assured him via FaceTime. "The consultant said that this was a warning for him to start taking things easy."

"Do you think he'll finally take early retirement?" he asked.

"Oh," she said, laughing. "You can count on it. Mum's read him the riot act. You know what she can be like when she's in that mindset."

Carter had to agree. His mum was one determined lady.

Thoughts turned to Maya and how he'd had to leave her behind. Worse than that, they hadn't exchanged numbers. A heavy sigh came from him.

"What's up, baby brother?"

He closed his eyes and ran a weary hand across his brow. Sally was very much like their mum and wouldn't give up until she had the whole story.

"Right, grab yourself a drink. This is a long story…"

"Oh, my goodness. It's like a cheesy romance story, isn't it?"

He laughed at his sister's statement after he'd finished his story. "It's exactly what we said."

"You love her."

Carter's eyes widened. "Is it *that* obvious?"

"Your wise older sister knows these things. There must be some way you can contact her."

"I know where she works."

"Cool, that's a start. Where?"

"The book publisher in town."

"No brainer then, Carter. After the New Year's break,

you can go and see her. Better still, why don't you call the hotel to speak to her."

"I never thought of that."

She laughed. "You're welcome, I told you I was wiser than you. Now just hurry home."

"On it. Can you pick me up at the station in say, an hour?"

"Sure."

MAYA

Maya was getting ready to go down for dinner and the party. She was wearing the dressing gown that Carter had worn. She inhaled his aftershave and his own signature scent. It was the closest thing she had to remind her of him. The phone rang in the room. She wondered if it might be Esme checking up on her. It was still a little early to head down to the bar.

"Hello."

"Maya."

That one word in that sexy voice brought tears to her eyes. Again.

"Oh God, Carter. How are you? How's your dad?"

"I'm okay. A little tired. Still at the hospital. He's going to be fine, but he needs to take it easy. Are you okay?"

The concern in his voice broke her and she wept. "No, I'm not. I miss you so much."

"Me too. I told my sister about us."

"What did she say?"

"Well, I got upset because I didn't know how I was going to contact you. She suggested I ring the hotel." He chuckled, his words sheepish. "I didn't even think of that."

"Neither did I. Poor Esme has had me crying all over her."

"I'm so glad you have them with you. But in this moment, all I want is you in my arms."

His admission made her heart beat a little faster. "Me too. I have an idea, but only if you want to."

"Go on."

"Let's exchange numbers and then we can FaceTime at midnight."

"Great idea!"

Once they'd exchanged numbers, Maya felt a little better. With a lighter heart, she got ready to meet her friends for dinner, already looking forward to seeing Carter, even if it couldn't be in person.

CHAPTER 14

After his call with Maya, his mood was considerably better. His dad was sleeping peacefully in hospital where he'd spend the next few nights under observation. His mum wanted to stay with him and so he'd gone back to stay with Sally and her husband, Mark. After dinner, they sat watching some Hogmanay programme. All he could think about was Maya's FaceTime call.

"Hey, only ten minutes to go," Sally teased him.

"Ten minutes too long," he mumbled.

After the countdown to the New Year and hugs with Sally and Mark, Carter heard his phone ring. He quickly answered it, and there on the screen was the most beautiful sight he'd ever seen.

"Happy New Year, Carter!"

"Happy New Year, baby." He heard his sister giggle in the background.

"Who's that?" Maya asked.

"My big sister who is determined to tease me to death for calling you baby."

"Can I talk to her?"

Carter smiled. "Sure. Just don't gang up on me."

"Can't promise that," Sally called out over his shoulder. "Hey, Maya, Happy New Year."

"And to you too. How's your dad doing?"

"He's okay, thanks. Our mum is with him. So, Carter told me all about how you met."

Carter grumbled.

"Is he whinging?" Maya asked.

"Yeah. He does that sometimes. I wish I'd witnessed the moment you two saw each other on the coach."

He heard Maya's laughter. It warmed him at how easy the conversation was between Sally and her.

"It was priceless. Trust me."

"I'd better hand you back to my brother before he has a freak out. I look forward to meeting you."

"Me too."

Carter took the phone back and went into the hall for some privacy.

"I wish I could be there to hold you. You look so beautiful."

"I wish you were here too, but I'll be home soon. Hang on, Esme and the gang want a word with you."

Carter loved catching up with them. He laughed as he saw they were all rather tipsy. He hated when the call had to end.

"Promise me we'll keep in touch until I get back home. I have our friends, but it's not going to be the same without you."

His heart burned. "Of course. Oh and, Maya?"

"Yes?"

"I hope Mrs Hungry and her husband don't keep you awake!"

She laughed. "Don't you worry. I fully intend to sing the Birdy Song at the top of my voice and do the conga outside their door later!"

MAYA

Maya zipped up her suitcase and prepared to leave her suite. She was sad that the trip was at an end but looked forward to meeting up with Carter again. The night before, she'd exchanged numbers with her four friends, text them to Carter and gave them his number.

While sitting on the coach, she heard Lisa's voice bubble up in panic. Sid was missing... again. She had to go back inside and get one of the staff to ring his room. Minutes later, he arrived on the coach, sporting the same Brexit top he'd worn most days. Mrs Hungry had taken double the amount she usually pinched from breakfast. The woman had enough for the whole coach to feed on.

The teens were still glued to their devices. They now looked a little less bored knowing they were returning to their friends. Looking across the aisle, she smiled with affection at Doug and Esme. She was looking forward to staying in touch and meeting up with them. As the coach pulled away, she rested her coat against the window like a pillow and fell asleep.

On the way back, the journey seemed much quicker, and it wasn't long before the coach dropped the first passengers off. Along with Esme and Doug, she was on the last drop off. The coach pulled up and they alighted together. Maya went to pull their cases out for them, but an arm held her back.

"Here, let me help."

That voice would always cause tremors of excitement in her belly. Carter. She cried out and flung herself into his arms, kissing him deeply, not caring who saw. Just being in his arms made her feel better.

"What are you doing here?" she whispered in a breathy voice.

A smile lifted his lips. "I thought you might need a lift home."

"Hello, young man. You're a sight for sore eyes." Esme smiled.

"Good to see you too. Do you need a lift?"

"No. One of our daughters is coming in a few minutes. We'll see you soon, though. Take care." Esme pulled him in for a hug.

After their farewells, Carter took Maya's case and headed over to the car park.

"Did you want to get something to eat?" he asked as the car pulled away.

"No, I'll be okay. We ate at one of the service stations on the way home."

They reached her home and Carter followed her into the house. They stood watching each other. It wasn't awkward, although Maya had to break the silence.

"Do you have to be going?" she asked.

"I have nothing I need to do. I've seen my dad today, just going to head home."

"Stay with me?"

A gentle smile broke through his lips. "If you want me to."

She nodded. "Cuppa?"

"Tea would be good, thanks. Do you have milk?"

"Yeah. My neighbour always gets me some when I'm away."

She busied herself in the kitchen, aware of Carter watching her. A pair of arms circled her waist and turned her around. Her eyes landed on his and her body trembled.

He placed one hand on her cheek. "I love you, Maya."

"I love you too," she responded without hesitation.

"I know it's crazy, but I've fallen deeply for you. I think it was as far back as when you chucked your coffee over me."

Maya laughed. "Not so far back for me. It was actually when I watched you with the oldies on our trip. Your caring nature. Oh, and your fit butt. Esme caught me ogling you," she admitted.

"Glad it's not just my body you want me for." He pulled her flush against his hard body.

"To hell with the cuppa. Come on, let me show you my bedroom. I need to be reminded of just how hot your body is."

"Fine by me."

New Year's Eve That Year...

CARTER

He sat on the edge of the bed, watching Maya as she slipped on her sexy deep blue dress. A dress which clung to each one of her delicious curves. As though sensing his eyes on her, she turned to face him. She walked his way, swaying her hips in a deliberately exaggerated movement. The one she knew drove him crazy.

He stood and placed his hands on her shoulders. "Damn, woman, you're so sexy. You make me want to…"

She placed her finger to his lips to halt words. "Stop it. It's taken me ages to get ready. We can celebrate New Year's later, after midnight."

He grinned and stole a kiss from her lips before she could protest. They broke apart and stared at each other for long minutes. Carter leaned in for another kiss and she pushed away from him.

"You are incorrigible." She headed for the door.

Carter was in hot pursuit and pinned her against it. "I know, but you love it."

They headed down to the hotel bar to meet with their friends. Friends they'd made on the same trip the year before. Although, last year, he'd gone home to see his dad who was ill. This year, he had plans to make it extra special.

He reflected on the past year and couldn't help his smile. After meeting Maya from the coach, he'd gone back to her home and they'd declared their love for one another. It hadn't been long before he moved in on a permanent basis. And three months ago, with their properties sold, they'd moved into their forever home.

A few days after their return from the coach trip, they'd

heard from the travel company. Due to the mix up, they'd been given a voucher for two hundred and fifty pounds each to spend on a trip of their choice. That choice had been the same coach trip, including staying in the bridal suite! It was a no brainer really, especially as their friends Esme, Doug, Annie, and Jean were going too.

Some of their friends had found it a weird choice, even when they'd explained how much fun they'd had. It was also where they'd found love with one another. There were a few other familiar faces, including Sid, complete with a new Brexit jumper with Boris Johnson's picture on the front. Mrs Hungry and her husband were there too. Fortunately, they were not staying in the room next to theirs this time.

Lisa the tour guide was there too. She was more relaxed this time, probably because the coach driver was also her new partner. They should call it the love coach. A hand tugging his took him away from his reverie.

"You were miles away." Maya's smile melted his heart.

"Just thinking about how we met and where we are now."

"Hmm, I still can't believe it either. Come on, our friends are waiting."

MAYA

Carter had been distracted the last couple of days of their trip. An air of nervousness surrounded him. This was certainly not normal behaviour for him. He exuded confidence as if he owned it exclusively. Maybe it was recalling his dad's illness the previous New Year. They sat with their friends having a pre-dinner drink. They'd managed to keep in regular contact with all four of them.

When they'd met Esme and Doug's daughters and their families for the first time, it had been lovely. All of them were most welcoming and as exuberant as their parents. It had been a chaotic affair.

She reflected on the cook offs she'd had with Carter. He could have seduced her with his dishes alone. She'd admitted it to him on one occasion and that had ended with them covered in flour while he *seduced* her against the kitchen counter.

They took their seats and ate their meal.

"It's not like you to play with your food, love," Esme noted while Carter pushed his food around his plate.

"Must be all the cream teas and extras I've had over this holiday." He didn't sound too convincing.

Maya put her cutlery down and rubbed his arm. "Are you sure you're okay?"

"Never better," he stated and kissed her cheek.

Midnight was fast approaching, and they headed for the centre of the dancefloor. Maya couldn't keep her eyes off Carter. He wore a full tux and looked so hot. She couldn't wait to strip him out of it later.

"Why don't you take your jacket off?" she called out over the music.

"Not just yet."

"You must be boiling. Are you certain you don't feel ill?"

The countdown started and then they all linked hands and sang Auld Lang Syne. Afterwards, there was much hugging and kissing. She turned her back to hug Esme and suddenly there was silence, then whispering. Maya cocked her head.

"You need to turn around, Maya," Esme instructed.

When she turned, her hand flew to her mouth and she gasped. Carter was down on one knee, with a small deep red satin box held out to her.

"Maya. Even after you threw coffee all over me and tried to mow me down, I think there was a spark between us. And after spending this trip with you last year, I knew you were the one. Maya Singleton, will you marry me?"

The silence was loud, even though she could hear a few excited whispers ripple through the crowd on the dancefloor.

She knelt in front of him. "Yes," was all she could manage to say through her tears.

He took out the solitaire diamond engagement ring and placed it on her outstretched shaky finger. When he put it on, he helped her up and kissed her so passionately that she almost slid to the floor. Cheers went up around them and then they were receiving many hugs and well wishes from their coach party and the other group too. They headed back to their table and looked in confusion at the bottle of champagne and six glasses waiting for them. They looked at one another and Carter shrugged, indicating that it wasn't him.

"I had an idea this was coming," Esme advised from beside them. "So, I ordered a bottle... just in case."

After sharing a glass with their friends, they said their goodnights. Now was the time for private celebrations. They called their families first, both sides ecstatic at the news. Maya watched as Carter took off his jacket and undid the bow tie.

"Need a little help?"

He held his hands open wide. "Take me, I'm all yours."

"Right answer," she murmured.

Who'd have thought finding her ex in bed with another woman would have led to this? One thing to thank him for. She undid Carter's shirt and frowned.

"What's up?"

"I was just thinking."

"Oh, a dangerous thing," he teased.

"Look, I know we love exotic foreign holidays, but…"

He tilted her chin upwards and she became lost in the depths of his green eyes. "But what?"

"Would it be nuts to have a winter wedding and…"

"And have our honeymoon on this same coach trip?" he finished for her.

She nodded, wondering if he thought the idea was daft. Then he broke into a huge smile.

"The best idea ever. Maybe our family might join us, and our new friends too?"

She reached up and kissed him soft and long, revelling in the warmth and love of this amazing man. Go on a coach trip? Find love on that coach trip? If anyone had told her that just over a year ago, she'd have laughed in their faces. But now… well, now was a different story.

ABOUT THE AUTHOR

Toya writes in paranormal and contemporary romance genres. A very important moment for her was giving a reader closure after surviving domestic abuse. It was after reading her Romance/Thriller, Flame, about a domestic abuse survivor, that she sent Toya a thank you message, and she's never forgotten it. "If it means I have helped one person, then I'm blessed."

Writing has been her passion since a very early age. Sadly, it wasn't until the death of her mum, who was also her best friend and biggest supporter, in 2009 that she started to take it seriously. Her mother's wish was to see her published, which didn't occur until 2014. Each book she publishes is dedicated to her.

When not writing, or reading her main hobbies are; cinema, theatre, live bands, gardening, keeping fit, Formula One racing, darts and spending time with friends. She lives in Suffolk with her husband, grown up son and Masai the cat.

Her mantra is "One Life, Live It."

www.toyarichardson.co.uk

Toya's Treasures is a new reader's group, she'd love to see you there.

TOYA'S TREASURES

www.mewe.com

Printed in Great Britain
by Amazon